D1483205

The Children
of Bird God Hill

Iris Macfarlane

The Children
of
Bird God Hill

illustrated by Robert Parker

McGraw-Hill Book Company

NEW YORK · ST. LOUIS · SAN FRANCISCO

For Fiona and Anne now grown up but once the children of Bird God Hill

First distribution in the United States of America
by McGraw-Hill Book Company, 1968
Text © Iris Macfarlane 1967
Illustrations © 1968 by McGraw-Hill, Inc.
All Rights Reserved. Printed in the United States of America.
First published in Great Britain by Chatto and Windus Ltd, 1967
Library of Congress Catalog Card Number: 68-30978

1234567890 VBVB 7543210698

Contents

one

The Day that Began It

IT ALL BEGAN with Beehu. Beehu was the big spring festival of Assam, a place in India, where Phyllida and Annabelle lived with their parents on a tea plantation. Also on the plantation lived three horses, a dachshund called Candy, a deer called Miranda, a parrot called Herbert—and an ayah. Ayah was a little Indian lady with a squint and tiny pink-palmed hands that flew to her mouth when she laughed. She had looked after them since Annabelle was born.

Ayah came from the hills and spoke a special sort of English and knitted all the time; walking, standing, sitting, her little hands clicked away at socks and sweaters for the endless relations she had left in the mountains of her home. When she was not knitting, or reading her Bible, or cooking herself spicy curries, Ayah was tidying their room, washing their shorts, and trailing after them as they galloped on their ponies down the paths between the tea bushes.

"You not going too fast," she would wail, "you falling, hurting lots, breaking backs, eberyting."

If they stopped to listen she would tell Phyllida and Annabelle stories about children she had known who had fallen off horses and spent the rest of their lives on their backs in plaster casts. Ayah had known a lot of children, and horrible things had happened to all of them. They had stepped on snakes in piles of dead leaves, put their heads into hornets' nests, fallen into disused wells, and got lost in the jungle where there were demons, or "bhoots," who buried you head downward, and fed on your toes.

When Phyllida told her they were going to spend Beehu with the cook's wife in her village she let out one of her highest pitched screams.

"Not going billage," she squeaked.

"Why not?" asked Phyllida who was nine and spending her last summer in India before going to England to school.

"Tigers," said Ayah. "Lots tigers. Bats big like dis." She stretched her arms, a knitting needle in each hand, to show the size of the bats that lived in an Assamese village. "Dey sucking blood. Liking white peoples too much," she added darkly.

"Pooh," said Annabelle who was eight and permanently pretending to be a horse. She had to take a rubber band bit out of her mouth to say "pooh," and to add "tigers and bats coming nighttime. We going day times, silly," before she whinnied loudly and cantered off toward the stables where the real horses were kept.

Phyllida and Ayah followed her, for it was seven in the morning and they always had a cup of tea with the syce, who looked after their ponies, before they went for their ride. It was the best time of the day, still cool, the air full of wood smoke and the smell of dung and hay. They drank tea out of bamboo mugs and wriggled their toes in the warm ash of the syce's fire, and listened to the green pigeons mewing like cats in the rubber trees.

In between mouthfuls Annabelle licked the bran off her arms where it had stuck when she mixed the ponies' food, and Phyllida scraped the edge of her mug with her penknife, and they both thought about the tigers and the blood-sucking bats.

"Why you going billage?" Ayah insisted. "I not going."

"You weren't asked," said Phyllida rather rudely. "The cook's wife asked *us*. It's Beehu, that's why. They're going to dance and have a feast and wash the cows and—lots of other things," she finished secretively.

"Hindu peoples," said Ayah scornfully, "Mummy not letting you go."

"We asked her and she says we can, so there."

*9

Phyllida was even ruder, because though she would not admit it, the tigers and the vampire bats had taken some of the pleasure from the thought of the visit. Ayah now added that there were wells in every village which were haunted by the ghosts of dead babies who had fallen into them.

"Pooh," said Annabelle again, dribbling tea down her shirt. "Who cares about silly old ghosts?"

In fact when Beehu came their heads were full of tigers and bats, and Ayah did not help by saying goodbye to them gloomily, as if she never expected to see them again. As they bumped slowly in the car over the rough track between the rice fields, the driver added some more ghosts to the wells, but said this was not the time of year for tigers or demons, who would be celebrating spring themselves. They spoke to the driver and to all the other servants in their own language. They did not think of him, or the cook, or the malis who were gardeners, or the sweeper who brushed, or the bearers who dusted, as servants. They were friends who made them kites, and fishing rods, and bamboo houses, and ladders of twisted creepers.

As soon as they arrived their fears vanished. The village was a square pond full of lilies and ducks, around it were little thatched houses with shirts and pumpkins spread out on the roofs. When the first welcomes were over they were caught up into the

Beehu day's business: the washing of the cows, the giving of presents, the eating of rice cakes and bananas green as parrots, the crushing of sugar cane between big flat stones; and in the evening the dancing and drumming by the side of the pond. This was the best part of the day, the air full of the smell of the spices for the feast that followed; and it was during the feast that Phyllida first saw the picture of the blue god.

The picture hung in the room where they were eating. They sat on bamboo mats on the earthen floor and scooped up golden curry in their fingers, and from the wall the god smiled down on them, a blue god who danced with a flute to his lips. Around the picture hung a garland of marigolds and above it a lamp, and the blue figure danced so delightfully in his circle of flowers that Phyllida stared at him in a trance. After a while the cook's wife came over to explain who he was. His name was Lord Krishna, and he was especially busy in the spring, piping the leaves from the trees and the rain from the sky.

Phyllida wanted to know more about him, so the cook's wife squatted beside her, and while they ate she explained how Krishna was brought up in a village house just like this. As a boy he and his friends would lead the calves of his father's flock into the forest of Brindaban nearby. Every morning they

*11

would set out with their flutes and their sticks, and their midday meal of rice and curds, to graze the calves. The forest was full of flowers and animals, of peacocks and ponds of wild duck. Brindaban was made for a god to grow up in.

As he grew older Krishna became a magical flute player. When he sat in the forest with a flute to his lips the bees stopped their humming to listen, the flowers bent their heads and swayed to his music, and all the animals were drawn from the thickets to lie at his feet. Tigers and deer, wolves and mongooses and snakes, they lay side by side in the grass at his side. Peacocks spread their feathers for him, and silly chattering monkeys crouched quietly against the golden sides of tigers who were their enemies. He was their god too, of course.

"Of course," said Phyllida. "How beautiful Brindaban must have been. Go on."

"Well," said the cook's wife, "he grew up from a handsome boy into a handsome man, and then it was not only the animals he charmed. All the milkmaids became sick for love of him, and when they heard his flute they left their churning pails and ran to him, to the forest or to the banks of the Jumna River, to dance with him the whole night through. On the full moon of the night that marked the end of summer he danced with them a wonderful last dance,

12*

their shadows leaping on the sands of the river bank while owls and frogs and jackals sat yellow-eyed in an awestruck circle around them.

Then he left them, for the time had come to start his work in the world. He was a milkman's son no longer, but a god come to earth to help the weak and overpower the wicked. When the milkmaids looked into the mists of early morning they could not find him. They followed his footprints along the river bank and into the forest, asking the birds and the trees news of their beloved, but Krishna's dancing days were over. He had other work to do."

"And so have I," said the cook's wife, preparing to get up and bring more food.

Phyllida was still with the weeping milkmaids by the banks of the Jumna River, searching in the white morning mist for the footprints of the one they would never find.

"So," she said at last, "what happened then?"

"So he continued his other work, helping the poor and rescuing princesses and fighting wicked demons. Whenever anyone was in trouble they called on him, and he came."

"*Anyone?*" asked Phyllida.

"Anyone," said the cook's wife firmly. "Anyone at all. He is still doing it. Perhaps one day he will help you."

"But I'm a Christian."

The cook's wife laughed and said that did not matter. Krishna loved all the world's creatures.

"One day when you are alone in the jungle you may meet him," she said, getting to her feet. "Then you will see."

Phyllida stared at the dancing Krishna enclosed in his golden garland, sucked the curry off her fingers, and sighed. There was little chance, she thought, being nine, English, and a Christian. She would probably never even hear the sound of his enchanted flute.

She did not know then how soon she would hear it, nor where it would lead her.

two

The Discovery

ALL THROUGH May they played the village game. The malis built them a small bamboo hut by the side of the pond in the paddock, and here they cooked rice, slapped their clothes on a stone at the water's edge, and laid them on the roof to dry. Herbert the parrot perched on top of the hut too and twisted the wet cloth in his beak, and Miranda the deer came mincing on her little pointed feet to share the rice.

They planted shrubs and two coconut trees and laid a lawn. From the clay by the side of their pond they shaped pots and baked them in sawdust, filling them with water, which they carried on their heads. They wanted silkworms and a loom. They wanted to grow rice, and for this most of all they wanted a pair of bullocks.

"Well, just one bullock," they pleaded with their mother at breakfast, "a small one."

They ate breakfast on the front veranda among

pots of trembling ferns with golden drops of dew plopping from the roof into the gutters. Mrs. Gordon sprinkled lemon juice on her slice of papaya and sucked her fingers thoughtfully. Her fingers were usually scratching in the garden, or else running through her curly gray hair to try to keep it tidy. She was dressed in a shirt and slacks as always. When she went into town, she changed into a cotton skirt.

"A small bullock would be just as much trouble as a big bullock," she said at last, but firmly. "Two ponies, a foal, a deer, a dog, and Herbert are quite enough."

"Talk of the devil," said Mr. Gordon. "Here is Herbert. Off with you sir! Back to your quarters this minute!" He waved a table napkin at the parrot who took no notice, but stood perched on the edge of the table with his eyes fixed on the butter dish. Mr. Gordon was a very tall, broad, red-faced man, but Herbert was not at all frightened of him or of anyone.

"But how can we plow?" complained Phyllida.

"Dig," said her father heartlessly.

"*Dig*," they squeaked together.

"Dig," repeated Mr. Gordon. "Good for the figure. The malis will help."

"It would take months," said Annabelle. "A bullock could do it in. . . ."

"No bullock," Mr. Gordon said in a final tone of voice. Annabelle kicked the table leg.

"You'd think we were asking for a tiger," she muttered.

"Look, Herbert's in the butter," said her mother. "Shoo! Scat, Herbert!" She too shook her napkin, and Herbert turned to her, his ruff up, his eyes popping from his head.

"He looks more like a major general than ever," said Mr. Gordon. "Is that the way to behave in mess, sir? By gad, I'll have you court-martialed!" He banged the table by the butter dish, and Herbert flew to the back of Annabelle's chair. He tweaked out some bamboo and sat glowering at them with the bamboo sticking out from each side of his face like a waxed moustache.

"And to think he's a *her*," giggled Phyllida. Whenever they thought of this it made them laugh till they cried. For the moment the bullock was forgotten.

"Lots to do," said Mrs. Gordon when they had wiped their eyes and Herbert had flown off in disgust to join his friends in the rubber tree. "We're going to study the life of Moses in school this morning and I must get some materials to make a basket. And look, there's Miranda eating my African daisies."

"She likes them," said Phyllida.

18*

"So do I," said her mother, and ran down the veranda steps and out into the garden. "Off you go, you little wretch." She gave the deer a gentle push, and Miranda shot away, galloped three times around the tennis lawn, and stopped short next to Mrs. Gordon and Phyllida, who had followed her.

"Mummy!" Phyllida said reprovingly, "you must never push deer. They hate it."

She leaned down to kiss the top of Miranda's sleek head, but before her lips had touched the silky fur it had shot away from under her mouth and Miranda was on her way to beating her previous record on the lawn. They watched her fondly.

"She is very beautiful," Mrs. Gordon said. "Not as pretty as when we got her, not as fluffy. But more graceful now, more elegant and gay."

"She's longer and darker and bonier," Phyllida said thoughtfully, "and I love her much more."

"Don't love her too much," Mrs. Gordon said, bending to pick the daisies Miranda had left unnibbled. "She is only a guest with us, you know."

"What do you mean? We're not going to let her go?"

"Not if we can help it, but wild animals are hard to satisfy because we can't really understand what they need. There's always something slightly troubled about them. And sooner or later they give in."

Phyllida stamped impatiently.

*19

"Mummy what do you *mean?* Give in to what?"

"To whatever happens. Illness, or the urge to go back to the jungle, or trusting the wrong people. We can protect them up to a point, but they always seem to go beyond it in the end. Try not to love her so much that you will be dreadfully hurt when she goes."

"You can't help loving a thing," Phyllida protested. "You can't suddenly just *not*."

"No, you're right, once you've started you have to go on, and often you don't even know when you have started. Love sort of steals up on you, doesn't it? The thing to remember is that dying is often the most comfortable thing that could happen."

"Oh, no," Phyllida shook her head violently. "Miranda isn't going to die. I won't let her."

"You can't decide what's best for her," Mrs. Gordon said, and then to change the subject she pointed at a great sweep of parrots overhead. "To think they're all Herberts," she said. "Suppose they all landed on us like visitors from Mars. We would be ruined. We would have to eat our meals in sealed rooms, and wear padded shoulders, and make butter till our arms fell off. It would be ghastly."

"I would love it," said Phyllida. "I would love to have every bird and every animal living here with me."

20*

"You're not doing too badly," her mother remarked.

Which reminded Phyllida of the bullock again, but her mother was as firm as ever, and in the end it was the old mali who solved the problem.

He arrived one morning looking very sheepish and leading two small, knock-kneed but undeniable bullocks. He also brought his plow, and the sight of these sent Annabelle galloping around the lawn whinnying shrilly. Phyllida tore off to ask if they could skip their school lessons just today. Their mother said she supposed so, because bullocks were an unexpected blessing that did not turn up every day. Even Ayah was quite impressed and went off to prepare pints of lemonade to stave off the sunstroke she knew they would get even through their bamboo hats.

They spent most of the day behind their bullocks, twisting their tails gently to direct them, crying "Gooriya gooriya," as they plodded through the sticky mud. Sweat poured down their faces and turned into streaks of brown as they rubbed it off with muddy fingers. The earth furrowed stickily like half-cooked chocolate pudding, and egrets ran leggily to collect the worms and frogs they were turning up.

By tea time the small square was finished. They led the bullocks to the pond to wash them, and to feed them some of the ponies' bran. They watched their thin sides, furrowed like the earth, hoping to see the dents between the ribs fill out.

"If they were ours," said Phyllida, "we could have them fat in a week."

"When we sell the rice we can buy one," said Annabelle.

"Gosh," said Phyllida. Then she looked gloomy. "Rice takes months to grow," she reminded Annabelle. "We won't be cutting ours till November and we're going to England for Christmas."

They thought glumly of the prospect of leaving India, their ponies, Miranda, Herbert, and Candy; and then of the idea of buying a bullock again.

"If we had some silkworms we could spin and sell silk," said Phyllida.

"If we had proper pots we could sell those," said Annabelle. "If we had a wheel."

"If we had a factory we could make tea," said Phyllida. "And tennis balls from the rubber trees. *If.*"

But before they had a chance to solve the problem of earning bullock money, Annabelle became ill and their parents decided that her tonsils must come out. She left for the hospital with their mother, the checker board, two tray cloths to embroider, and six skeins of silk with their black and gold paper still unbroken; and it was while she was away that Phyllida remembered the blue god and made the discovery.

At first Phyllida felt busy and important. She had the ponies to look after, and she must watch the birds to see what berries they were feeding on so that she could collect them for Herbert. She must dig clay for pots and water the coconut trees; and her mother had left her with two maps to draw and the eight and nine times tables to learn.

For three days all these things kept her busy with a happy frown on her face. Then suddenly she felt lonely. She had not realized she would miss Annabelle so much. It was a missing that started when she woke up and there was nobody in the bed beside her, snoring, that continued through the morning, without anyone to kick under the schoolroom table. It lasted through the hot afternoon when they usually rested and Annabelle snored and she was able to rid herself of boredom and temper by saying "baby, baby, fancy sleeping in the daytime." It settled on her most heavily in the evening when they became villagers, absorbed in their work of watering and pot-making and their dream of bullocks.

The June days were steamy and sweet-smelling, for all the flowering trees were out, and the court-yard of their little hut was pink, gold, and scarlet with fallen blossoms. Phyllida sat there on the

*23

morning of the fourth day since Annabelle and her mother had gone, and trailed her feet in the water of the pond. Miranda was browsing in the paddock, her coat like syrup in the morning sunlight. Parrots were shrieking in the rubber trees, among them Herbert with one ear cocked for the breakfast bell. The first butterflies were out, pale lime-colored flutters of cloth among the cassia blossom. It was very beautiful, and Phyllida was lonely.

She looked at the hut with her head on one side, trying to decide what to do with it next. The lawn was growing, the coconut trees were growing, the shrubs and hedge were growing so fast you could almost see them. Storm clouds massed behind the hills each evening, like an army of elephants. Sometimes there was the rattle of thunder, but the monsoon rain had not reached them. When it came the rice would grow fast, so they would plant it then.

They would have a small celebration she thought, at the time of the planting, asking for the blessing of God on their crops. They would light butter oil lamps and place them on the altar; but, Phyllida remembered, we have no altar. That was wrong, of course they must have an altar. Every village house had one. She must find some bricks and make it quickly.

She shook the water from her feet and put on her tennis shoes. Bricks, she thought. Now where could she get bricks? Ayah came sauntering down, knitting as she walked, and Phyllida asked her advice. Ayah shrugged. There were a few broken pieces behind her house, she thought. Phyllida did not want broken bricks. She wanted nice ones, she said, whole and perfect because she was going to build an altar.

Ayah's palms flew to her mouth.

"Mummy cross you do dat," she said.

"Why?"

"White peoples not do like dat," said Ayah, as she said about everything interesting they suggested.

"They do if they like," Phyllida said. "Don't we have altars in our churches?"

"Mummy tink you getting Hindu," said Ayah firmly.

"Mummy not know," said Phyllida, who did not want to work out whether she was getting Hindu or not. Certainly it was the blue god she thought of now, and pictured fluting on her altar. But she did not tell Ayah this, and she would certainly not tell her mother.

The breakfast bell rang, and while she ate her puffed rice and shooed Herbert off the butter, she was thinking about bricks. She jumped when her father said:

"I'll be going to the brick fields this morning. Like to come along?"

"Could I have some of the bricks?" Phyllida asked casually.

"Good gracious, what for?"

"For a—thing I'm making."

Her father did not think she could have new bricks, and offered her broken ones from the factory, but these she politely turned down. Somewhere, she suddenly remembered, she had seen—of course, the ruin! On a hill a mile from the bungalow was what remained of Bird God Hill temple, a ruin full of beautiful, shiny flat tiles, Assamese tiles made with the whites of ducks' eggs, Ayah told her. They would be perfect for her altar, but how could she collect them? It would take days to plod up and down the hillside with bags of tiles. Then she remembered where she had seen some others like them.

She thanked her father and said she was too busy to go with him to the brick fields. He looked surprised and asked her if she were lonely and she said "Gosh no," hardly able to wait to be rid of him before calling Candy and setting off to find her tiles.

She had first seen them when she was looking for berries for Miranda. She had wandered down a little path in the jungle beyond the paddock, not far because of the bhoots who buried you head downward, and had noticed the tiles half hidden by undergrowth and mud by the side of the path. That day she had collected the berries and hurried back, with only a casual glance at them. Now she took a canvas bag and tore along the path without a thought for Ayah's warnings of what was lurking in the jungle. She was afraid the tiles might have gone.

They were still there, their pointed pink corners sticking out of the earth. She bent down to poke at one with a bit of stick, but it was too firmly embedded to be moved.

"Bother," she said to Candy, "I should have brought a spade."

Candy was busy digging.

"Here," said Phyllida, "Dig here, Candy. Dig these up for me."

Candy did not even hear as she snuffled and yelped excitedly. Phyllida looked to see what she had found, but it was only an ants' nest. Soon Candy's nose was covered with ants and she was sneezing and shaking her head.

"I'll get them off for you," Phyllida told her, but Candy squeaked and ran off into the long grass, her tail between her legs.

"Silly," Phyllida called after her. "Come back here or you'll be eaten by a leopard."

She poked at the tiles again, but decided she would not be able to get them out without some sort of tool.

"Candy," she called, "Come on, I'm going back."

*27

89740

Candy did not come, and though she did not really think the little dog would be eaten by a leopard, Phyllida did not like to go back without her. The jungle was thick for a couple of miles before it opened out into tea bushes again, and she might run around in circles and get lost.

"Candy!" she shouted, "Can-dy!" Still no dachshund, and Phyllida stamped impatiently. "You naughty girl," she bellowed. "Come here this minute."

One minute, two minutes, three went by, and Phyllida began to be worried. Perhaps the ants were a very bad kind, and were stinging her to death; or perhaps in her fright she had fallen into a hole or gotten pierced by a bamboo.

At the thought of the terrible things that might be happening, Phyllida's eyes filled with tears. Sobbing "Candy, Candy, where are you?" she plunged into the tangled grass and ferns.

It took a long time to force her way through the snapping bamboo and stinging grass. As she pushed and crawled she called "Candy, Candy" in gasping sobs, at every step more convinced that something had happened to her. She grasped a plant with a thorny stem and as she let go it sprang back and hit her in the face. She put her hand to her cheek and found it was bleeding, and the blood, mixing with her tears, made her feel desperate.

"Ow," she moaned, "My doggy, my pet . . ." and stopped dead in her tracks.

The jungle had suddenly thinned and opened into a small glade. There was a hump in the center of the glade, and on the hump, leaning over at an angle but still complete, was a little brick temple. Digging frantically at the base of the temple was Candy.

Phyllida stood, staring. It was so unexpected, the lost temple in the jungle, that for a moment she forgot all her fears for Candy. It was a little beehive-shaped building with carvings around its roof, and creepers crawling up and over it in every direction. There was a big tree beside it, whose roots seemed to have tipped the temple over; or perhaps an earthquake had done it.

It looked quaint, a little silly, leaning over to one side like that, with the creepers lashed around it as if to keep it from falling. The tears dried on her cheeks as she suddenly knew what she would do. She would make this her altar, her secret, private place of worship. She would tell no one about it, not even Annabelle. It would be absolutely hers.

Delicious shivers of excitement ran down her spine as she planned it all. She would have to be very careful and clever about coming here. She would clear away the weeds and creepers, scrape off the moss, and somehow she would get an image of Lord Krishna. She would bring butter lamps and flowers for him, and perhaps one day he would step out of the jungle, beautiful and blue with his flute to his lips. . . .

She stood for some minutes, imagining this scene, until Candy, tired of her digging, came and danced up and down in front of her.

"You naughty dog," said Phyllida dreamily, but bent down to kiss Candy's muddy nose. "You're not naughty really," she confided. "You're very clever to have found it. If it weren't for you I would never have known."

She stepped up to the temple. Its door was so overgrown that she could only move the tangled stems aside and peer in. There was nothing to see except darkness. A dank smell filled her nostrils. "Bats," she thought, and for a moment a tiny pulse of fear beat in her throat. Could this be a devil's temple and not a god's?

She drew her head back from the door, and her courage returned. It was such a happy, sunlit glade, the temple so delightfully askew, so round and fat and pot-shaped; it couldn't be haunted by bad spirits. In fact here she would be safe from them, here under Lord Krishna's protection.

She shook herself free from another dream and looked at her watch. It was half past nine. Ayah would have finished her washing and be coming to look for her.

"Come on, Candy, quick," she called and plunged back the way she had come. This time she did not notice the grass that scratched her legs and the twigs that caught in her hair, and it seemed no time at all before she was back in the paddock. She was only just ahead of Ayah, however.

"Hebens, where you been?" Ayah greeted her. "You all muddy, bloody."

"Candy running jungle-side," Phyllida said casually, glad that she was telling the truth, if not all of it. "I go fetch."

"T'cht." Ayah shook her head at Candy and gave her a friendly slap. "You bery naughty dog. I telling not to go jungle-side. Lots tigers, Nagas. Nagas eating dogs."

Candy danced up and down on her little back legs and waved her paws as if she were swimming. She was very muddy too, and bore out Phyllida's story.

"Come," Ayah said briskly. "You getting clean, putting Dettol on cuts."

With her arm around Phyllida's waist their heads were nearly level. "Mummy sending letter," she added.

The letter said that Annabelle's tonsils were safely out, but that she was pale and crotchety and a week in the hills would do her good. If Phyllida would like to come to the hills too, of course she was just to say so.

"Lubly," said Ayah, whose relations lived there. "Lubly cool. Going, not?"

"Not," said Phyllida, and she explained how she had to stay with her father and look after the animals.

Ayah pouted and tried to persuade her, describing her auntie's house where there were bees which made beautiful honey, and a waterfall with a pool at the bottom in which she could swim. But Phyllida knew what she wanted to do with the precious days before a suspicious, nosy Annabelle returned. Ayah could go to the hills and see her auntie's bees, she said sweetly; she must stay.

"You staying, I staying," said Ayah with a resigned sigh, and went off to cook herself a sizzling curry to relieve her feelings.

three

The Footprints

THE BEST TIME to visit the temple, Phyllida knew, was after lunch when Ayah slept, and the malis dozed in the shade of the hedges, and her father drove off in his jeep to tour the tea garden. She was supposed to sleep too but she seldom did; she lay on her bed reading and drawing and watching the lizards stalking insects on the white walls. From half past one until four nobody would know that she was not on her bed.

The only difficult part would be to cross the garden to the paddock for there was a chance, in spite of the dozing malis, that she would be seen. However, that was a risk she must take. She could always pretend that she was going to see Miranda; and so that this story would not be a lie she did look in on the little deer as she passed. Miranda, sleepy-eyed and breathing heavily, did not bother to get to her feet.

*33

On that first afternoon Phyllida's heart pounded in her throat all the way down the stairs—she used the back staircase—and around the edge of the tennis lawn; and only quieted when she was safely in the paddock. She squatted in the grass by Miranda's side and wiped the moisture off her forehead with the back of her arm. The worst was over for the moment; even if one of the malis had seen her she felt sure no more would be said. The malis were her friends.

When her heart was quiet she slipped across the paddock and through the little gate that led into the jungle. Her first anxiety was whether she would be able to find her way back to the temple. Perhaps the grass would have grown so fast in the rain that the half-hidden tiles would now be completely lost in it. But no; after only a couple of minutes she found them.

She turned off confidently and began to push her way through the creepers and branches as she had done the day she had been following Candy, but after a few minutes her anxiety returned. The first time she had stumbled on the temple, but how could she be sure she would do so again? In this thicket there were no landmarks; she might be walking in a different direction. Her heart sank at the thought of losing the treasure she had so recently found.

Then she remembered the big tree whose roots had tipped the temple sideways, a peepul, the sacred tree whose figs she had often collected for Miranda. If she could see that, it would lead her to her lost treasure. She looked around, but the grass on all sides was too tall to see over. She must climb up onto something. Slippery bamboo stems were no use, she must find a tree. She pushed forward impatiently, hating to think that the precious time was passing, and that the temple was so near, yet so hidden. Then, as suddenly as the first time, it was in front of her.

It was as delicious as she remembered it: better, she decided, more mysterious in the hot hushed midday silence, more peaceful and refreshing. The tree above seemed to be throwing protective arms around it, and the little glade was filled with contented shadows and patches of gay sunshine. A faint breeze stirred the pointed peepul leaves and whispered a welcome. We have been waiting for you to come back, the leaves seemed to be saying. We have been waiting for so long, for hundreds of years, for you to find us. There is so much for you to do, so much for you to do for Lord Krishna.

"So much to do," Phyllida said out loud, and stepped forward. So much to do but where to start? First she would explore the temple thoroughly inside and out, and then she would be able to decide. She walked up to the door and rather gingerly pulled aside the tangled undergrowth.

In the strong afternoon light the darkness within was not as solid as the first time she had been there. She could see that there were carvings along the walls, set into little alcoves, and faint chinks of light showed that there were windows that were almost blocked. If she could let more light in, it would make her work much easier and the thought of the bats less hard to bear. She stepped out into the sunshine again, and walked around the outside of the building to look for windows.

She judged, from where she had seen the light, where the windows should be, and started to pull aside the tangled growth of leaves and stems. Soon, excitedly, she felt her fingers slip through and knew that she had been right. She pulled and tugged, forgetting the heat, cutting her finger joints with the tough stems and forgetting that too. This was a window all right, but not just an ordinary one. It was a flower window, a lotus window, the centers of the stone petals hollow to allow the light to penetrate. When she had finished clearing away the weeds she stepped back to look at it.

It was very small, two feet square, or perhaps a little more. The flower was framed in stone, delicately; the petals almost looked wind-blown even though they too were stone, and several inches thick. She ran to see what the inside of the temple looked like, now that the light could find its way through, and was enchanted. There was a gold lotus of sunlight on the floor at her feet, and already the smell of the bats was less strong. Once she had cleaned all the windows the bats would go, and she would be left with flowers of sunlight and the real flowers with which she would fill it. Lord Krishna would not be able to keep away.

She stood in a trance for several seconds, happy in a way she had never been before. She was to get this feeling every time she came to the temple; a deep throbbing content that made her aware of the ground under her feet, and the air around her, and the trees and the sky, as if she were part of them. It was as if she were about to step into an enchanted country, new, but deeply familiar. She came out of her trance slowly, collected her arms and legs about her again, and started slowly but steadily to pull away the weeds and creepers from the walls.

For a week she worked on the inside of the temple. She found as she cleared that the carvings were of wavy flowers, and there were two short-legged elephants and a figure with an umbrella over his head. On her second visit she took a bamboo brush to sweep away the dust and cobwebs, and by the end of the week she had cleared all four windows. She took a trowel too, and as she scraped and emptied her trowel of mud, and scraped again, the floor glowed up at her a deep and shining red, just as it must have looked when it was first made.

She longed for water and for polish to rub on the red tiled floor. She wanted a long brush to clean the roof. She would like a can of whitewash. Nevertheless every time she stepped through the door and saw the gold lotuses of sunlight on the glowing tiles, the fat little elephants, the mysterious figure under the umbrella, and the wall curving protectively around her to meet in a shadowy point above her head, she felt the same contentment.

Now she needed flowers, she decided, and butter lamps, and an image. She could bring flowers, and water for them in a bottle. Butter lamps she could buy for a few annas in the bazaar, or perhaps there would be a few in the cow house left over from last year's festival of lights. The image was the difficulty. She knew exactly what she wanted: Lord Krishna with his flute to his lips as she had seen him in the picture. With half-closed eyes she pictured the image as it would look in the alcove opposite her, the blue figure glowing softly in the light of the lamps. She would bring jasmine and frangipani blossoms and place them around it; but the day after tomorrow Annabelle and her mother would be back from the hills and the secret would be harder to hide. Still, tomorrow was Sunday; she could buy an image in the bazaar.

She rose stiffly from where she had been sitting, resting with her back to the wall, and looked at her watch. It was time to go home. Time, which lay like a lead weight on her when she was resting in bed, flashed past when she worked at the temple. She hid her brush, took one last look around, and stepped out into the sunshine. Then her heart almost stopped beating.

All around the temple, fresh and clear in the red mud, were footprints. They had not been there when she arrived. Someone had walked silently out of the jungle, and around the temple, and away. Whoever it was must have seen her as he glided barefoot past the windows. But she had seen no shadow, heard no crack of twig.

She bent to examine the prints. They were small, not much bigger than her own; but she was wearing sandals, so there was no question of confusing them. They disappeared when they reached the grass so she could not tell in which direction the visitor had gone. She had no doubt at all as to who it had been. Like the milkmaids beside the river Jumna, she knew Lord Krishna's footprints when she saw them. He had come to see how she was getting along with his work.

The thought floated her home, so that she hardly

felt the ground under her feet, and the scratching grass was like silk against her legs. It kept her glowing all through tea, and while she groomed and fed the ponies, and weeded the garden of their hut. The duller the jobs she set for herself the more contented she grew. It was as if one of the butter lamps she was going to light in the temple was already burning with a steady flame inside her.

The flame only went out when she could not find Miranda. At first she did not worry too much. Miranda could melt into her surroundings in the best deerlike way, and it was often hard to separate her from a dappled patch of sun and shadow in which she was sitting. But usually she was hungry for her last meal, and came bounding to Phyllida with squeaks of pleasure.

"Miranda. Su-pper," called Phyllida, but no glossy galloping figure emerged. She walked slowly around the big run, peering under bushes and into hedges, but there was no stretched neck or pricked ears, no neatly folded knees. She began to get anxious.

She searched the run again, lifting every leaf and parting each branch, but there was no doubt about it. Miranda had gone. Somewhere, somehow, she had escaped. Phyllida tried not to panic, but she felt a little sick as she ran to the gate of the paddock and across the lawn.

"Daddy, Ayah, mali, sweeper, everybody," she called. "Come quickly, Miranda's escaped."

Faces appeared, footsteps clattered.

"She can't have gone far," her father soothed. "She must be in the garden."

They divided the garden into sections and each searched and called, but there was no Miranda. At last her father found a corner in her run where the joined wire had been pushed apart. It was a small corner gap, but big enough for Miranda's narrow body to go through. When he showed it to her, Phyllida burst into tears. Beyond the hole in the wire grew the jungle, the same patch of jungle in which her temple lay hidden. They could search for a month and find no trace of Miranda, but a hungry leopard would sniff her out in a night.

"It's too late to go on looking for her now," said her father. "I'll have some men search for her in the morning, but I don't mind betting she comes back on her own. She won't find milk and bananas ready for her whenever she wants them in there."

He was wrong, however. Miranda did not come back, nor did the men who beat the jungle discover a trace of her. Phyllida was afraid they might find her temple in the search, but the next afternoon when she went to put the image in its niche, all was undisturbed. The image was not the dancing figure she had hoped for, but a seated one, white and peaceful, one arm across the folded knees. It looked very beautiful among the butter lamps and jasmine she had taken. Sun-splashed, flame-flecked the temple glowed, and the still white figure seemed to come to life—the smile on the calm face to widen, the fingers raised in blessing. Phyllida stared wide-eyed until a golden blur spilled from the lamps and washed over her.

"Miranda will be all right if she stays here," she said softly. "This is enchanted ground."

She bent forward to touch the footprints as she left; they were still clearly visible in the red earth.

"Take care of her, Lord Krishna," she said, "and send her home soon."

four

Midnight in the Jungle

ANNABELLE returned the next day, thinner and paler and talking in a new high voice with a strange accent.

"Why do you talk like that?" Phyllida asked her.

"Lake what?" said Annabelle, "Ay'm talking ordinarily."

"You're not," Phyllida assured her. "Your voice is all high and funny and you say 'Ay' instead of 'I'."

"Ay do not," Annabelle said crossly, her eyes beginning to fill with tears. She cried a lot during the first week, and only had the energy to kick Phyllida half-heartedly, and did not bite her once. She was particularly annoyed that there were not dozens of pots ready for them to sell.

"What have you been *doing* all this time?" she wanted to know. "Ay've made three tray cloths and you haven't done a thing."

Phyllida, who had forgotten about the bullock in her excitement over the temple, said, "I've been looking after your horses, that's what I've been doing. And watering the rice and weeding and—oh, thousands of things."

"You didn't look after Miranda very well, did you?" said Annabelle nastily; and then she regretted it, because Phyllida's eyes filled with tears too, and they both howled dismally at the thought of Miranda lost.

It was the afternoon and they were resting, Phyllida wondering how she could escape to the temple. Soon Annabelle would sleep and she could go, she thought, sniffing into her pillow. And while she thought, and sniffed, tired with heat and sadness, she too fell into a deep sleep. While she slept she dreamed.

She was at the temple on a moonlit night when the whole world was milky white. She was sitting outside the temple by the side of a small lake, and on the other side of the lake, leaning over to drink, was a little silver deer. She knew this was Miranda, and as she sat with her plaster-white arms across her knees, watching the deer's neck curve over the water, she felt relief flood over her.

"You aren't lost," she said to Miranda in the dream. "You're here and you're safe. I've found you and nothing can hurt you."

"Wakey wakey!" sang out Ayah's voice. "All sleeping peoples wakey wakey."

"Stop it," bellowed Annabelle into her pillow. "Me sleeping. Leabing alone."

Phyllida blinked. She took in the hot room, the green light filtering through the drawn curtains, Ayah, the peacock fan on the wall, and turned on her face. There was no moonlit temple, no lake, no lapping deer. Once more her tears ran into her pillow, and she took a lump of it in her mouth to stifle her sobs. She sucked and chewed at the salty cotton in an agony of disappointment.

It was only later, when she thought of the dream again, that a memory stirred at the back of her mind. Sometime or other Ayah had told her that prayers and presents offered by the light of a full moon would always be acceptable. It was a "bery lucky time," for Christians as well as Hindus. At tea time her mother said "Full moon tonight, we must remember to look at the moonflowers," and the words seemed to come to her as a message.

Full moon! The "bery lucky time" when prayers would be, must be, answered. The time of her dream, the time when she and Miranda and the temple would be together in the silver world she had so clearly seen. She must go to the temple tonight and say the prayers, and enter the milk-white miracle.

After tea she went down to the little hut and sat

on the edge of the rice patch. The seedlings were a foot tall; soon they would be ready for replanting. But for once Phyllida stared at them without interest, in fact she did not see them. She saw instead the gate that led from the paddock into the jungle. She saw her own hand opening it and her eyes staring along the moonlit path ahead. She saw deep shadows, and the glitter of eyes. She heard owls and rustles—footfalls. She felt bats' wings, the slimy bodies of snakes, and a cold hand on the back of her neck.

"I can't, I can't," she whispered, her fists clenched, and her throat tight, at the thought of that midnight walk to the temple.

"But I must," she argued to herself. "I must do it to save Miranda. What's the use of having a temple if I don't pray in it?"

"I could go tomorrow, it probably isn't true about the full moon," the frightened half of her pleaded, "but I went yesterday and that wasn't any good, was it?" argued the determined Phyllida.

Then she thought of her dream and the cotton wool content in which it had wrapped her and of the certainty it had left in her mind that she and Miranda and the moonlit temple were linked in some magic unexplained fashion; and she made up her mind. She would take a flashlight, some rice and spices, and fresh flowers, and she would pray in the temple that Miranda would meet her there. She would pray by the light of the round, most auspicious moon.

She felt happier as soon as she had decided. She dug away the dam and watered the rice, and then slapped the mud back into place and stamped it with her bare feet. She squatted by the side of the seedlings and ran her palm across them. Their tight-packed glowing greenness comforted her. What a celebration they would have for the cutting of the first rice. Perhaps she would take Annabelle and show her the temple. Yes, she would do that. She would have cleared the whole glade by then, and Annabelle would not be able to claim an inch of it.

The most difficult part of the plan, Phyllida found, was to stay awake until the rest of the household was asleep. It had been easy enough to get saffron and curds for the offerings, and oil for the lamps. Frangipani flowers she could pick on the way. She fingered the flashlight, and felt under her pillow for the handkerchief full of rice and spices, and the jar of curds. She felt a little sick and very sleepy. She decided to count up to five thousand very slowly to stop herself from falling asleep. She got as far as two-hundred and sixty-three.

She awoke with a bar of moonlight across her eyes, and at once she realized where she should be.

*47

What time was it? How long had she been sleeping? She looked at her watch, half-hoping it would be nearly morning, but the hands stood firmly at half past eleven. She jumped out of bed and slid on her shoes, her shorts, and shirt. She wanted to go to the temple, she told herself, her teeth chattering. If only the jungle did not lie in between!

Candy jumped out of bed too and her nails clicked up and down on the wooden floor of their room. Annabelle turned over and groaned.

"Ssh," said Phyllida, and dumped the little dog back onto her bed. "Stay here, good dog. I won't be long."

Candy whined and rubbed herself along the bed on her stomach. For a moment Phyllida wondered if she would take her as protection, but decided against it. Candy might run back and awaken the others.

She slunk along the veranda and down the front steps. The garden was flooded with moonlight and loud with crickets. An owl boomed like a foghorn and frogs clacked to each other across the pond. There were fireflies below and a million stars above and the air was sickly-sweet with the scent of moonflowers. She paused at the foot of the steps to look at them—a dozen dangling heads, their paper petals wide and trembly, moon dazzled. She picked one of the blossoms to take as part of her offering, though she knew that in an hour it would be dead. When she passed the frangipani tree she added three waxy flowers to her bouquet. She breathed their fragrance deeply before putting her hand on the gate into the paddock.

She stopped at the pond, suddenly remembering the lake in her dream. Could this have been where she saw the silver deer? But there was no deer, and with a thumping heart she crossed to the gate that led to the jungle. Before she opened it she turned on her flashlight. It was a small one, and the faint gleam it gave was soon lost in the wide night. For one long moment she hesitated, overcome by the longing to run back across the lawn, up the stairs and into bed beside Candy. Then she opened the gate.

The first hundred yards down the path were not too bad. The moon shone strongly, and she switched off the light to save it. She kept her eyes fixed on the ground in front of her; she knew if she turned to stare into the thick black grass beside her, she would see shapes. If only she could stay on the path! If only she did not have to turn and walk through that terrible grass!

It was even more terrible when she entered it than she had imagined. It seemed thicker at night as it pressed against her like hands, like claws; it breathed cold wet breath on her cheeks. Each time she put out her hand to clear her path she expected a figure to loom ahead, a skeleton figure with caged ribs and hollow eye sockets and great hooked fingers to clasp her wrists. . . .

"Dey liking white peoples too much," she heard Ayah's voice in her ear. "Dey liking white peoples, dey liking white peoples. . . ."

A sudden rustle in the bushes stopped her, rigid with terror. Pretend to be dead, she told herself, lie down and pretend to be dead. But she could not move, her knees would not bend, her eyes would not close. She stood in the middle of the path unable to breathe, ice cold and soaked in sweat.

"I can't go on," she thought. "I can't, I can't."

"But I'm nearly there," she told herself. "It's easier to go on than go back. I can't go back."

Slowly, inch by inch, she lifted the flashlight and shined it into the darkness ahead. She should be able to see the temple by now, but she could see nothing but hostile breathing grass. In front, behind, around, it hedged her in. It seemed thicker than ever now, just when it should be thinning out. Where was the peepul tree? Where in fact was the path?

She took a few shaky steps ahead, then whirled around and looked back.

"I don't know where I am," she whispered hoarsely. "I'm lost."

Impossible, she could not be. Every day for two weeks she had been taking the same path. She knew exactly the bend at which she must turn off, and her feet had smoothed the way so securely that she had often said to herself, "I could find my way blindfolded." Yet now, by flashlight and moonlight, she had blundered.

She was lost in the jungle at midnight. If she screamed nobody would hear, except the bhoots and the leopards. She remembered stories of men who had walked in little circles until their tongues turned black. She would not last that long. She would be dead and her bones picked dry by vultures before her father had been able to arrange a search party.

A clatter in the branches above emptied her of all feeling. She stood, a white weight in the jungle path, unable to look up or down, fixed by fear as if there had been a stake down her spine. But no writhing length of snake fell on her, no leopard snarled. How long she stood there she did not know, nor how much longer she would continue to stand. She seemed to have lost the power of controlling her legs, and even if she could move them, which way should she go? Back? Which way was back? Had she turned completely around, or only imagined she had? She thought of other stories of men who had gone mad from nights spent alone in the jungle.

Then she thought of something else. She cleared her throat of the cotton wool that filled it.

"My Lord Krishna," she whispered, "my Lord

Krishna, I am lost. Please help me find my way. Please help me. Please."

Her tiny voice was drowned in the cricket calls and the owls' hooting. He would not hear. Besides, she was a Christian, so why should he answer her calls, since he had so many lost Hindus to help?

"I cleaned the temple for you," she pleaded. "Take me to it, please. I am lost."

And then she heard it, unmistakable, familiar, enchanting—the sound of a flute. The notes dropped onto her head like a hand in blessing. The terrible feeling of loneliness, of helplessness in a savage world, left her. Instead she was surrounded, protected, accompanied. She did not see the blue figure with the flute to his lips, but she knew he was there. His presence made the jungle voices sweet. Fear fell away from her.

Without the slightest hesitation she turned toward the music. It led her back the way she had come, and then, as she had known, it drew her along to the peepul tree, the glade, the moon-washed temple. She ran the last twenty yards, certain that here would be the blue figure, the flute player.

But the temple was quiet, and the music had stopped. Strange, she thought, and stepped inside the door. It was pitch dark but she was not afraid. Krishna might not show himself to her, but he was here and she was utterly at ease in his company.

"I will light all the butter lamps, and then I will give you your presents," she told him. "I'm afraid the flowers are squashed, but I'll give you better ones tomorrow."

She took matches from her shorts pocket and lit each lamp in turn. The image, cream in the circle of flame, smiled at her. She placed the drooping flowers beside it, and then drew from her pocket the handkerchief and the cold cream jar.

"Bother," she thought, "I should have brought a brass bowl for my offerings."

She looked around but there was no place to put them. She went out into the white glade, picked two large leaves, and hurried back with them. Tomorrow she would bring brass bowls and fresh flowers. There should be incense too, to carry her prayers to heaven. However, she did not need it now, since god had so compassionately come to earth to her.

"All I ask," she said as she knelt in front of the offerings, "is please bring Miranda back. If you will do that for me, I will do anything for you. I just want Miranda safe."

She stared at the smiling image, half expecting it to speak. For a long time she knelt, waiting for something—for the click of deer hooves on the tiles, for the notes of a flute. But nothing happened; no voice spoke except the shouting crickets.

Then she thought of her dream and how she had been sitting with her back to the temple wall when she saw Miranda. If she sat like that again maybe it would come true. Anything could happen on this most miraculous of nights, including a lake where now there was nothing but grass.

She stepped outside and sat down in the position she remembered from her dream. Through half-closed eyes the dappled glade did look like water. She slid lower, until one elbow was supporting her. Yes, it looked very much like water, pale trembling water, moon-milky water. Her eyes closed and her elbow slid down under her head.

Yes, it was a lake, and there, curving above it, spreading silver ripples as she drank, was Miranda. Phyllida sighed in her sleep.

five

The Footprints Explained

SOMEONE WAS tickling her feet and ankles.

"Ayah," Phyllida grunted, "stop doing like dat."

"Annabelle," she groaned a few seconds later, "shut up. I'm cold, cover me up."

But nobody answered and the tickling went on. Slowly she swam up through the silver lake, where she had been swimming with milkmaids and Miranda, and bent down to pull up the sheet over her legs. But there was no sheet; instead her fingers met a hard, furry head. She opened her eyes with a start and sat up.

"Ow," she groaned, for the arm on which her head had been resting would hardly straighten; but she forgot this in the surprise of finding she was not in bed. She was still lying outside the temple, and Candy was licking the dew off her legs.

The glade was full of bird song and gray morning light. Great golden drops of dew plopped from the

roof of the temple onto the sodden grass and a black
and yellow spider lay stretched out in a web of
swinging seed pearls. She had been out all night.
The strangeness of it, the wonder, kept her crouching quite still against the temple wall, while Candy
licked and licked, uttering little whining noises of
pleasure and distress.

"You naughty girl," said Phyllida at last, coming
really awake and swinging her legs gingerly. "How
did you get here?"

Candy jumped onto her lap and put her paws on
her shoulders, licking her neck and ears. Phyllida
looked at her watch. It was just after five; nobody
would be awake. She would have time to get back
into bed without being missed. But how could she
explain her sodden clothes, her scratched legs, and
Candy's muddy stomach? She had better pretend
she had been out for an early walk; it was true in a
way.

She got stiffly to her feet and stretched. She felt
wonderfully rested, as if she had slept all night in her
comfortable bed at home, instead of in the middle of
a jungle full of wild animals and bhoots, sodden with
dew and chewed by mosquitoes. Of course she had
been safe in the protection of the temple, as far as
wild animals were concerned; and thinking of them
she remembered the purpose of her visit: to find
Miranda.

She looked around. Now there was no lake, no deer, nothing but grass and bird song and strengthening sunlight on the shining peepul leaves. Nevertheless she felt in some way comforted about Miranda. Her journey through the night could not have been in vain. If there was no lake here there was one somewhere else, where Miranda was safely drinking. She felt quite sure of this. She bent to pick three leeches off her ankle, called to Candy, and after a quick look inside the temple, turned for home.

Then she suddenly stopped. The moist earth outside the temple where she had seen the first footprints bore, unmistakably, the signs of new ones. The flute player! He had been here as she knew he must have been, out of sight but watching over her. His prints led around the temple and then started toward. . . . She caught her breath and Candy gave a couple of squeaky yaps, for standing at the edge of the glade looking down at her from wide, dark brown eyes, a bow and arrow over his shoulder, was a boy.

They stared at each other in silence for several seconds and then the boy stepped into the sun and smiled. His teeth were as white as new-peeled sticks, his skin was golden brown, and his black hair had a strong reddish tinge. It was very wild and looked as if it had never been brushed. He had a flat

*57

nose and large ears and was half a head taller than
Phyllida. He was dressed in a ragged pair of shorts
and was very dirty.

"Who are you?" said Phyllida at last, putting a
hand on Candy's neck to stop her springing forward
and snapping at his ankles.

"I live here," said the boy with a vague nod over
his shoulder.

He must be a boy from the houses where the tea
pluckers lived, Phyllida thought, out hunting for
squirrels. How terrible that he should have stumbled
on her temple.

"How did you find this place?" she asked.

"Oh, I have known about it for a long time," said
the boy. "I often come here."

"You do?" Then she looked at his bare feet
and the puzzle of the footprints was a puzzle no
longer.

"Are those yours?" she said, pointing at the prints;
and he said yes, they must be, for as far as he knew
nobody else could have made them. Phyllida felt a
stab of disappointment, but then she considered the
chances of a god leaving footprints and decided they
would be small.

"This is my temple," she told the boy rather
loudly. "I found it and I'm keeping it a secret. You
will keep it a secret too, won't you?"

"I have known about it for a long time," said the boy. "I have known about its secret."

"Its secret?" It seemed that as well as being her secret from everyone else, the temple had one of its own.

"Oh yes," said the boy calmly, walking over to lean against the wall beside her. "My grandmother told me about its secret."

"Your grandmother knows about it too?" said Phyllida uneasily. It seemed that half the world was aware of what she had been so carefully hiding.

"Yes, and she knows the secret."

"Won't you tell me?" asked Phyllida. "I won't tell anyone, I promise."

"Myself I do not know it," said the boy. "Only my grandmother knows. She says she will tell me before she dies."

"Oh." Phyllida did not want his grandmother to die, but she would dearly have liked to know the secret. "And who else knows?" she asked. "Does your grandfather know?"

"I have no grandfather."

"Does your mother know, or your father?"

"I have no mother or father," said the boy. "I live with my grandmother."

"Oh dear," said Phyllida, "I'm so sorry. How do you live? Where do you get money to eat?"

"My grandmother spins," said the boy, "and she makes medicines and spells. She knows all about the bhoots who live in this jungle, and she makes spells against them. We have a cow too, and some rice land. And I shoot."

"I see." Phyllida thought for a moment about all this and then she said politely, "I hope I will meet your grandmother." In fact she sounded a fearsome old lady, rather like a witch, but perhaps useful to know with those spells against bhoots.

The boy walked up to the door of the temple and peered in.

"Why are you doing all this?" he asked. "I have been watching for the last week. Why do you want to clean this place?"

"Well . . ." said Phyllida. Then quite suddenly she found herself pouring out the whole thing—how she had wanted an altar, how she had found the temple and discovered about the blue god, how she had felt this was a specially wonderful place and had wanted to keep it as a sort of hiding place. "A sort of sanctuary," she finished, the idea dropping into her mind as if it had been ready and waiting.

"Sanctuary?" asked the boy.

"A sort of place where everything can be quiet and safe. Even wild animals. The Lord Krishna used to tame wild animals in the forest of Brindaban. I thought he might do the same here."

It did not sound very convincing, but the boy seemed to understand.

"I can bring you animals," he said, his eyes lighting up. "My grandmother can help with her spells."

"Well. . . ." said Phyllida doubtfully. "I didn't mean to collect them exactly. I thought if I made a sanctuary they might come on their own. My deer too, which I've lost. You haven't seen a barking deer, have you?"

The boy said he hadn't, but he would look for Miranda. He spent most of his days in the jungle, collecting plants for his grandmother's spells and for them to eat, and shooting whatever he could for food.

"You won't shoot here, will you?" Phyllida pleaded. "That's the whole point of a sanctuary. All the animals can feel safe in it."

"I could bring you so many animals," said the boy wistfully. "I could make you cages for them too. I could bring you a black monkey with a white face and squirrels and a snake as big as this whole space." He indicated the length of the glade, which was about forty feet. "I could tell you so many stories about them, I know everything about animals. I know how they speak and everything."

Phyllida pictured the glade full of white-faced monkeys, squirrels, forty-foot snakes, deer, and baby leopards, and maybe an elephant. Then she sighed.

"It wouldn't be fair to catch them," she said. "They would have to be hurt or something. Then we could feed them and nurse them till they became strong."

"Ah, there are plenty of wounded animals in the jungle," said the boy, "and little ones whose mothers leave. Birds too. I could get you plenty."

"Could you? Could you really? And we could make a garden for them and they could play and grow strong together."

Already she could see the squirrels tripping up the backs of the snakes, and tigers rolling over in the speckled sunshine with baby deer between their paws. "Gosh!" she exclaimed, "it would be super." Then a thought occurred to her. "But I have school," she said. "I could only come in the afternoons. Who would get their food and look after their wounds and everything?"

"I would," said the boy. "And my grandmother. She knows the medicines for all the wounds in the world."

"And at night?"

"I would build strong cages," said the boy. "They would be safe."

"Specially here with Lord Krishna," said Phyllida. She stared dreamily around the glade which was now full of morning sunshine. The bamboos had stopped weeping golden tears and butterflies were whizzing about, busy over breakfast.

"Breakfast," said Phyllida out loud. "Heavens, I must go. They'll be sending out searchers for me." She turned to the boy and joined her hands against her chest in the Indian way of offering greeting or goodbye.

"This is our secret, isn't it?" she said solemnly. "You and I and your grandmother. Nobody else must know."

"Only my grandmother," promised the boy. "Because she knows already. She knows more than we do. When will you be back?"

"I'll try and come this afternoon. If not, tomorrow. Will you be here?"

"I will be here," said the boy, and without saying goodbye he turned and slipped into the jungle.

"Come on, Candy," said Phyllida.

She knew she would get into trouble when she got home, for going off without telling anyone, and for coming back in such a mess; but she was too happy to care. As she made her way home along the jungle path she thought back over the night and the morning, and decided she would never be afraid again. The jungle might be mysterious, but its mystery was kind. It was part of the magic that she had heard falling out of the night in the notes of a flute.

six

The First Animal

SURPRISINGLY she did not get into trouble. Ayah wrinkled her nose at the dirt and said "Tcht, you always bringing trouble upstairs." And Annabelle had gone riding.

It was a bit of disappointment that her great adventure was so calmly ignored. She was bursting to boast of it, and the more she thought of the temple and of all the plans she and the boy had made for it, the more she felt that Annabelle should share them.

Though they fought about nearly everything—the chair they sat in at meals, the pony they were to ride, who was to have the first of the mulberries, the leechus, the peaches, who could jump highest, run fastest, stay under water longest—though from every dawn to dusk they never stopped arguing, yet they had always shared important secrets.

Apart from anything else it would be much easier

if Annabelle knew; it would be hard to deceive her, but together they could put up a stronger defense against Ayah and their parents. Besides it would be another pair of hands to help clear the temple, tend the animals, another tongue to talk about it all, and another brain to solve its secret.

"I'll ask the boy this afternoon," Phyllida said to herself as she gingerly washed her scratched legs before breakfast. "If I don't die of malaria first."

She did not die of malaria, but instead of going to the temple after lunch, she went to sleep, more tired than she knew by the excitements of the night. When she awakened Annabelle was already dressed and washed, her long yellow hair tied in ribbons on top of her head. Her mother would not let her braid it like a horse's mane.

"Fancy sleeping all day like a baby," said Annabelle when she awakened, getting back for all the times Phyllida had said this to her. "It's five o'clock and you've been snoring like a pig for hours."

"Pig yourself," said Phyllida, who was exceedingly irritable, from the sleep, and because of the time she had missed at the temple. "Dibs I ride Ginger."

"I dibsied ages ago while you were snoring like a. . . ."

Annabelle did not get out "pig" because Phyllida threw a pillow at her, but instead of hitting her it hit the glass of orange juice that Ayah was carrying in to refresh them. Ayah screamed and the glass fell to the floor and splintered. Candy started to lick up the juice and both Phyllida and Annabelle screamed and leaped at her.

"You always fighting, always fighting," Ayah moaned. "Odder childrens not doing like dat. Maureen, Bobby, dey neber fighting." Maureen and Bobby were the children Ayah had looked after before she came to Bird God Hill and they were, according to her, perfect. She was always telling of the white socks they wore, and the teeth they never stopped cleaning.

"Candy eating glass going *dead*," Annabelle shrieked, and she pried Candy's mouth open to see if there were any splinters in it. Candy choked, wriggled from her grasp, and fled from the room with her tail between her legs.

"Me getting cloth," Ayah said resignedly and she went off muttering that Maureen and Bobby never spilled orange juice or threw pillows.

"Stupid bores," giggled Phyllida, wide awake with all the commotion. "I wish those hornets had stung them to *death* when they stepped on their nest."

"I wish all the snakes in Assam had wound around them and choked them while they were wearing their white socks," hooted Annabelle.

"I wish their teeth had fallen out crash with all

that cleaning," shrieked Phyllida. "Crash crash crash into the wash basin, and gone down the drain."

The picture of all these terrible fates overtaking Maureen and Bobby had them rolling on their beds in paroxysms of laughter, kicking their legs in the air.

"Gosh," gasped Annabelle when she could get her breath. "Look at your legs."

"What's wrong with them?" sniffed Phyllida.

"The bites. Millions of bites. Where on earth did you get them?"

This seemed a good time to tell her about the temple, but just at that moment Ayah came back with a cloth. It was not until she had slowly wiped up the broken glass and the juice, and had told them of a child she knew who had swallowed some glass and had to eat a plateful of cotton wool sandwiches, and had gone off again with dreadful warnings about not walking with bare feet, that they could return to the subject of Phyllida's legs.

"I got them in a special place." Phyllida spread her legs in front of Annabelle importantly. "A secret place. I was there all night."

"All night? What night?"

"Last night."

"You were out all last night?" Annabelle said. "Bosh."

"It's true," Phyllida said haughtily. "You needn't believe it if you don't want to. If you don't want I won't tell you any more about it."

"I want to know," Annabelle said in a humbler voice.

"You've stopped saying 'Ay' instead of 'I'," Phyllida suddenly noticed. "Your voice is quite ordinary again."

"Tell me about this place," Annabelle said impatiently. "When did you find it? Why haven't you told me before? Where is it? Why is it so special?"

Before Phyllida could answer any of these questions Ayah had returned once more to tell them that tea was ready and to go down on her hands and knees to search for any slivers of glass she might have missed.

"Glass bery bad ting," she complained. "Going foot, foot getting bad, dropping off."

"I wish Maureen's and Bobby's feet had dropped off with their white socks on them," said Phyllida, and ran out of the door before Ayah could reach her.

"H'm, h'm, h'm." Annabelle neighed for the first time since her tonsils came out. "And fallen into a deep muddy puddle so that the white socks got all green and slimy like spinach soup."

Spinach soup was the thing they hated most, and it

cheered them a great deal to think of Maureen's and Bobby's socks in this condition.

They giggled about it on and off all through tea, which was waiting for them on the veranda: bread, butter, tomatoes, and sponge cake. Mrs. Gordon was removing a couple of ants from the sugar bowl when they joined her.

"Animals everywhere," she complained. "They treat this house like a sanctuary."

Phyllida spluttered and tomato juice spurted over her shirt.

"A sanctuary?" said Annabelle.

"A nice safe place where they can stretch themselves out in the shade and have three meals a day. There isn't an inch on which some sleepy bloated creature hasn't settled down to spend his life at my expense."

"I wish it were a real sanctuary," Annabelle said. "Couldn't we. . . ."

"No, we couldn't," her mother said. "We couldn't provide beds for Himalayan bears, and there isn't room for an elephant in Daddy's study, and I don't want a tiger sharpening his claws on my sofa."

"Tigers are terribly tame . . ." Annabelle began, but stopped when Phyllida kicked her under the table, and mouthed, "My secret," dribbling more tomato juice and wiping it off on the back of her arm.

Her mother told her to use her handkerchief and while she was wiping her mouth Annabelle said, "spinach soup," which sent them both into spluttering laughter, and sponge cake crumbs from Annabelle's mouth flew across the table.

"For heaven's sake," said their mother. "What on earth's got into you? Finish your milk, Phyllida, and then you can go."

"Oh, must I?" Phyllida hiccuped. "It smells."

"Smells? What of?"

"S-s-spinach soup," she whooped, and for several seconds they both laid their heads on the table and howled with helpless laughter.

"It's high time," said their mother when they were sniffing quietly again, "that you were both at school. Boarding school I mean."

"Then we shall have to eat everything that's put in front of us, I know," said Phyllida. Her mother always produced boarding school at difficult moments. She drank her milk holding her nose as if it were medicine.

"I shall starve myself to death," she said between sips.

"Good," said Mr. Gordon, who had just joined them. "Fewer bills for me to pay."

"You look tired," said Mrs. Gordon.

"And you're sopping wet," said Annabelle.

"I am both hot and tired. This is the busiest

month of the year if you remember. The tea is growing about an inch a minute and I haven't nearly enough hands to pluck it."

The bearer brought him a large glass of water which he drank without drawing breath.

"And why were you going to starve to death?" he asked Phyllida, when he had finished it.

"Boarding school," said Annabelle, "boring old boarding school. Mummy said it's high time we went. We said we'd starve ourselves to death if we did."

"You'll love it," her mother assured her.

"Without horses?" Annabelle asked incredulously.

"You can have riding lessons every week."

"I can ride perfectly well, I don't need lessons," Annabelle said haughtily. Then after a moment's pause, "With jumping?"

"Yes, if you like. On big horses, full size ones."

"Fifteen hands?"

"Heavens," said her mother, "I don't know. Just ordinary size horses."

"And can I have a hacking jacket and a hard hat?"

"I suppose so if Daddy has enough money after buying name tapes and ten pairs of everything."

"If Annabelle has a hard hat I jolly well want ice-skates," said Phyllida. "Long fancy figure ones. White."

"Ye gods!" exclaimed their father. "I'll have to work till I'm seventy-two to keep the two of you in hard hats and figure skates."

"When you're seventy-two we'll be about fifty," said Phyllida. "We'll have husbands to keep us then."

"I won't," said Annabelle. "Ugh!"

"You'll have lots of nice friends your own age at school," said Mrs. Gordon brightly. "Won't you like that?"

"No, I jolly well won't," said Annabelle. "I shall hate it. School!" And she made another noise as if she were going to be sick.

"Oh, well," her mother said vaguely, "I'm going to de-tic the cows now. Anybody like to come and help?"

Phyllida looked at Annabelle and shook her head. It was a tempting idea but they had important things to discuss. They said they were sorry but they must exercise the ponies, and could they please go.

"And I must go and weigh my tea," said Mr. Gordon. "I think we shall have a record amount of leaf today. We'll need a bumper crop if I'm going to pay for all those hacking hats and ice-skates."

"And skating jackets," said Phyllida.

"And prayer books and paint boxes and pillow cases," said Mrs. Gordon.

"And socks like spinach soup," tittered Annabelle. This sent them both into gales of laughter again, and their mother told them to take their silly jokes off to the stables. It was not until they were out for their ride that they were able to talk privately about the secret.

Then Phyllida told the whole story as she had told it to the boy, and Annabelle said "Gosh" and "How super" at the right intervals, and "What a pity about Miranda," and several times "You might have told me before" in a grieved voice.

"I wonder what the secret is that the boy's grandmother knows," she said at the end. "What's his name?"

"The boy's? I don't know, I didn't ask him. He's from the workers' lines. He can speak to animals and all sorts of things."

"It was probably him playing the flute," said Annabelle.

"Of course it wasn't. In the middle of the jungle in the middle of the night? Don't be silly. Anyway no human being could play like that."

"You really think it was Lord Krishna?"

"I'm sure it was."

"Well, you must be a Hindu," Annabelle announced.

"Not necessarily," Phyllida said stiffly. She had thought about this several times, and had not been able to work it out about Jesus, whom she believed in, and Krishna, whom she had almost met. Would she have to discard one for the other, and if so which? "Krishna likes Christians," was the best she could offer to Annabelle. "He doesn't mind who's lost as long as they're lost."

"I bet it was the boy," said Annabelle, kicking the sides of her pony so that it broke into a creaky canter.

Later, when they were unsaddling, Phyllida said, "I won't show you the temple at all if you don't believe any of it."

"If you don't show me, I shall tell Mummy," said Annabelle.

They stared at one another, each measuring how serious the other was. Phyllida knew that Annabelle was longing to see the temple; but she also knew that she could and would follow her there. Annabelle realized that even if she found the temple it would lose half its magic if she disclosed it to her mother or anyone else. She wanted, as much as Phyllida, for it to be the sanctuary they had planned, with its secret that was theirs alone to discover.

"I believe some of it," said Annabelle. "Most of it," she added gruffly. "Can we go tomorrow?"

"If you swear you'll never tell Mummy or anyone else."

"I swear."

"Swear that if you tell anyone the bhoots will catch you and feed on your toes."

Annabelle swore this rather reluctantly.

"I don't think they'd want your dirty toes," said Phyllida comfortingly. "So don't worry."

Annabelle flung a handful of bran at her, and Ayah, who had just come up with her knitting, said, "You always fighting, always fighting. Me getting new childrens."

So the day that had started for Phyllida in such a magical fashion in the gray glade, ended in a bran fight and a hair wash, but she was happy as she fell asleep. Keeping the secret to herself had been a terrible strain. With a last wish for Miranda she fell asleep, to dream of snakes which Ayah was trying to knit, though they wriggled off her needles as fast as she tried to make them into stitches.

Ayah herself was not altogether Ayah, she was more a witch who was juggling with the snakes, pulling out of her knitting bag grass and twigs which she tossed into the air with the knitting snakes, and which landed on Phyllida's legs to bite and tickle. . . . She woke with a start, but it was only her mosquito bites itching. She had concealed them while she was having her bath, so nothing had been rubbed on to ease them. She scratched at her legs until suddenly she was asleep again, and this time she did not dream.

The boy was at the glade before them next day. He was sitting at the temple door whittling at a bamboo with his knife. Beside him was a basket closed by a lid. Phyllida told Annabelle to wait behind a clump of grass while she warned him. The boy did not seem to mind that now a fourth person knew of the temple; but they all took a solemn oath that the circle was complete, that the secret was to be spread no further.

Annabelle inspected the temple, the image, the flower windows, with eyes suitably round with wonder.

"Gosh, it's better than I thought," she said. "It only needs cleaning."

"I've been cleaning it for weeks," Phyllida protested. "But it's awfully difficult on your own. You should have seen it when I started, it was just a mass of creepers and cobwebs and bats. You should have *seen* it."

"If we could find a spring we could wash it down properly," said Annabelle. "We could bring scrubbing brushes and everything."

"I know where there is a spring," said the boy.

"Show us," they said.

He led them from the glade down a small path which his own feet had flattened. And there right across the path ran a trickle of water, disappearing into the ferns and bamboos.

"It never dries up," said the boy. "We can make a pond and have plenty of water."

"Our animals can drink it too," said Phyllida.

"We can drink it," said the boy, and he knelt down and put his mouth to the ground, sucking up the water.

"We have to boil our water," Phyllida said primly, "but gosh, I'm thirsty. Seeing that water specially."

"Me too," said Annabelle, "seeing that water *specially*. Come on, let's. It comes out of the ground, it must be clean."

"It comes from a spring just in there," the boy said, pointing. "Come, I will show you."

He drew aside the whipping grass and creepers and the spiky bamboo stems, and after a few minutes he showed them where the water gurgled out of the ground. An orange butterfly was drinking before them, but when it had finished they knelt and sucked up the cold spring water, Annabelle letting a little trickle out of the corner of her mouth like a horse. It tasted better than any water they had drunk, earthy and important as it must taste to a thirsty butterfly, or to a tiger.

"Our animals will love it," Phyllida said, wiping her mouth and her grass-dented knees. "Perhaps we could bring it in pipes right into the sanctuary."

"I have an animal already," said the boy casually, stripping his stick.

They whirled on him. Where, they wanted to know? How big? How had he found it? Was it badly hurt?

"Come, I will show you," he said, and led them back to the glade and up to the basket at the temple door. There was no sign of life from inside.

"It is just a small animal," he said, shrugging. "It was lying on its back. One of its legs must have caught in something."

Very slowly he started to untie the grass strings which were keeping on the lid of the basket.

"It can't be a tiger," said Annabelle. "It's too small and quiet."

"Or an elephant," said Phyllida. "Help, I hope it's not a snake. Oh no, it can't be because of its legs. Is it a biting thing?" she asked the boy.

He had the lid open and was putting his hand into the basket quite carelessly.

"Not a biting thing," he said. He scrabbled about while they waited with their mouths open. Then he pulled out a large, inert tortoise.

"Oh," said Annabelle and Phyllida together, trying not to sound disappointed. The tortoise pulled in its head and legs and they stared at the shell and tried to think of something to say.

"It's an animal anyway," said Phyllida at last. "It'll do for a start. And it'll be easy to keep. Tortoises hardly move, do they?"

*79

The boy sensed their disappointment.

"Tortoises," he said, "are the cleverest animals in the whole jungle."

"Are they? How?" Phyllida had taken the tortoise and turned it over. "Oh yes, I see its sore leg. Poor thing, what shall we do about it?"

"I will bind it with a plant." The boy pulled from his pocket some leaves, and gently prodded the tortoise's cut leg out, and tied the leaves round it. "Now it will heal," he said.

They put it on the ground and it lay like a lump of stone.

"It doesn't look very clever to me," said Annabelle. "Perhaps its leg is hurting."

"They are cleverer than monkeys," said the boy, "cleverer than tigers. They only pretend to be stupid."

"What about snakes?" suggested Annabelle, but the boy thought the tortoise would be safe from snakes too if it kept curled up, and no big animal would bother to break down the door of the temple.

"Anyway," Phyllida pointed out, "there is Lord Krishna. Inside the temple is right in the middle of the sanctuary."

They put the tortoise into its basket, and the boy gave it some leaves to eat, and they placed the basket on the floor of the temple, in front of the image.

Then Phyllida looked at her watch and found it was time to go home, for as usual the afternoon had raced past. They closed the temple door with a strong bamboo pole and agreed to meet there next day.

"I will cut more bamboos for cages," said the boy. "I will spend the whole day here. I will start the pond for the spring."

They sighed, envying him his life without school, without meals to be sat through and teeth to be brushed and rests to be taken. Before they said good-by Phyllida suddenly remembered to ask him his name.

"My name?" He sounded surprised.

"Yes. You have a name, haven't you?"

"Yes, I have a name." He seemed shy talking about the subject.

"Well, what is it then? Mine's Phyllida. Hers is Annabelle."

"Ah." The boy kicked the earth with his bare toes, hesitating. Then he looked up and straight into her eyes.

"My name," he said, "is Krishna."

A Storm and a Fright

THEIR SURPRISE over the boy's name kept them quiet all the way home; and almost as soon as they were in, Ayah burst on them with news that distracted their attention. She was waving a telegram and her hair, normally neatly oiled and pinned into a bun, hung in an untidy pigtail down her back.

"My auntie going ill," she announced. "Bery sick. What to do?"

"Your bee auntie?" asked Phyllida. Ayah had many relations and they had never sorted them out.

"Not bee auntie," said Ayah, sitting on the edge of Phyllida's bed and reading them her telegram. "Listen. 'Come-quick-Auntie-bad,'" she read. "Dis my Mummy-Auntie, my truly Auntie."

"Gosh," said Annabelle. "You'd better go quickly then. She may be dead by now."

Ayah screamed softly and rocked herself backward and forward, her head in her hands.

"Silly dope," hissed Phyllida. "What did you want to say that for? Auntie not going dead," she comforted Ayah. "You going quickly quickly, she getting better."

"How I going?" Ayah demanded. "Who washing socks, ears, eberyting?"

"We washing," Phyllida promised. "Mummy washing. Dhobi washing." Everybody, she assured Ayah, would wash furiously all the time she was away seeing to her sick auntie. She was sorry for Ayah and the trouble that was taking her away; but at the back of her mind there was a wicked feeling of satisfaction. With Ayah out of the way their visits to the temple would be easier than ever.

Later she found that the same thought had occurred to Annabelle.

"We can go in the morning as well, instead of riding," said Phyllida.

Annabelle thought they should ride to exercise the ponies, but they could cut back after a canter and tie Ginger and Snowball to a tree at the entrance to the paddock. This would give them an hour and a half at the temple before breakfast if they got up early.

"Mummy might even let us miss school," said Phyllida, but without much hope. Even after the big earthquake when the lake had tipped up, and the hedges wriggled up and down like snakes, they still had to do their lessons.

In fact the long table under the gold-stemmed Japanese bamboos was a happy place, but now in the hot weather the air was heavy on their heads and their thoughts were forever wandering down a jungle path to where a boy called Krishna would be waiting. Green pigeons rustled in the rubber trees, and tiny tickly feet ran up their legs. Goats bleated. Doves cooed.

They did their Bible reading first. It was the story of the Pharaoh and the plagues. Phyllida half listened as she sawed at the edge of the table with her penknife. When her mother's voice stopped reading she opened her eyes wide to watch a crested woodpecker swoop across the lawn.

"Look!" she said, "I know a story about how it got its red crest."

"Very interesting," said Mrs. Gordon, "but what's that got to do with the Pharaoh?"

"It's a red Indian story."

"I don't want to hear it."

"I do," said Annabelle.

"Another time, we've spent far too long on the Pharaoh as it is. Now it's history. Page 54. Henry IV."

"I *hate* all these Henrys," said Annabelle.

"Well, we've got to do them so you might as well resign yourself."

"If we were Assamese children we would just drive

the cows and wind holy collars around their necks and feed them with rice cakes," said Phyllida dreamily.

"If you were Assamese children you would be looking after your little brothers and sisters all day long from the age of five," their mother told them.

"We haven't got any little brothers and sisters," said Annabelle.

"You would have if. . . . But this hasn't got anything to do with Henry IV. Come on, let's finish him up. You read, Phyllida."

They got Henry IV over with and then they colored a map of the world for geography and then it was recess. While their mother went off to see the cook, they drank lemon juice and talked in whispers about the boy. Phyllida thought he might be Lord Krishna himself but Annabelle said they would have to be Hindus to think that, and before they had time to carry this thought any further their mother called them back to the school table.

It was hotter than ever, and while Annabelle started Book V of her readers, Phyllida sat with her French book in front of her, watching the perspiration trickle down the crease in her elbow and make a small pool on the table. They must make a pool in the temple glade, she thought; and she arranged her eraser and two small pencils around the damp patch by her arm and imagined the peepul tree and the temple. Miranda would come to it, too, of course. She took out her penknife and started to scratch little pointed footprints from the edge of the table to the perspiration pool.

"Phyllida, stop playing and get on with your exercise," said her mother.

Phyllida unstuck her arm, sighed deeply, put her head down beside her book and closed her eyes.

I'm the worst-treated person in the world, she told herself. *My mother and father don't love me, they only love my little sister who has golden curls. They are going to send me away to live with a cruel housemother who will put me in a cellar full of rats.*

She said "housemother" to herself again and wondered if that was what she really meant. She was beginning to feel very sad, she thought she might even cry.

"Phyllida, are you asleep?"

She lifted her head with a start, leaving another damp patch on the table.

"It's so hot," she complained, "and I don't understand this exercise."

"It is hot," her mother agreed. "We shall have to move inside, I think. Let's just read about Theseus and the Minotaur, then call it a day."

Theseus held their attention, and they were crayoning pictures of the myth in their scrap books when their father arrived. He leaned over Phyllida's chair.

"What's that striped pig doing lying in a field of gum drops?" he wanted to know.

"That," said Phyllida, "is not a pig, and those are not gum drops."

"A bull's eye in a heap of confetti?"

"Daddy!"

"What then?"

"Can't you see what this is?" Phyllida crayoned fiercely. "It's got horns."

"A snail?"

"It's the Minotaur," Phyllida said. "Here's the twisty maze that Theseus followed, and these are flowers and that's Theseus and Ariadne."

"Ah, I see it all now. I like the girl friend's hat. Very chic."

"Can't you see what this is?" Phyllida crayoned crossed to the other side of the table and stared at her picture.

"My word, that's original," he exclaimed. "A lump of coal blowing soap bubbles."

Annabelle laid her head on the table and laughed till she hiccuped.

"No?" said Mr. Gordon seriously. "Well, a slice of Mummy's chocolate cake that's been in the tin too long and started to grow mushrooms?"

"Oh, oh," pleaded Annabelle, "don't make me laugh any more, I shall be si-hi-hic. It's the Oracle at De-hel-hic-phi."

"Of course, of course, it couldn't be clearer. That's a cliff and that's the hole where the Oracle lives, but I can't quite make out this cloud of white smoke."

"That's a voice," said Phyllida, leaning over the table and screwing her neck around. "The Oracle's voice. It's obvious."

"My voice isn't like that," boomed Mr. Gordon. "Mine is a big, black cloud of smoke."

"Mine is a thin, wispy, tired little streak," said Mrs. Gordon. "And nobody has listened to it all morning."

"Perhaps you would like a holiday," Phyllida suggested. "We shall be very busy washing while Ayah's away so if you like. . . ."

Of course they couldn't persuade their mother to give them a holiday, washing or no washing.

"Only if there was an earthquake big enough to crack open the ground and the school table dropped in and we were all smothered," said Phyllida bitterly, "only then would she stop teaching us."

That evening they were quiet and obedient, and allowed Ayah to give them an extra scrubbing to last all the time she was away; and they promised to be as good as Maureen and Bobby in her absence. She was to catch the early bus to the hills next morning, and did not know how long she would be away.

"Not to hurry," Phyllida said kindly.

"Stay as long as you like," murmured Annabelle, nearly asleep the moment her head touched the pillow.

"You not going jungle-side, falling off horse, cutting knife, going snake-place," warned Ayah as she said goodbye.

"Of course not," said Phyllida, her eyes closed and her fingers crossed.

Next morning they were up early. It had rained heavily in the night, as it did most nights in July, and there was a blob of blue and gold on every leaf tip. The lawn in front of the house was being hopped over and pecked at and swooped on by birds. There seemed to be at least a hundred mynahs moving over it; and blue jays and crows, noisy and quarrelsome; and solemn plodding spotted doves, and spry little magpie robins, striped like peppermint drops.

In the trees the parrots had already arrived, and orioles glittered like wax candles, yellow blobs in the green of leaves and parrots. Beyond the lawn and the paddock were the hills from which the Nagas tramped down on Sundays. The first range always reminded them of a great shaggy animal, lying like a guard to prevent the plains people from entering the world of mountains. Sometimes they felt they could almost run their fingers along its humped back, and through its green fuzz of hair. Today it seemed to have been rolling in cotton wool and not shaken itself afterward.

"Good morning, monster," they called to it as they cantered past. Apart from the shreds of cloud on the hill-beast's sides there was a bright cloudless sky overhead. They tethered the two old ponies to the tree near the paddock as they had planned, where they could graze without being seen.

When they got to the glade, they found the boy and the tortoise up and about. The tortoise had taken its head and legs out and was standing looking around rather shakily, like a very old lady at a tea party. The glade dripped with colored dew and parrots were in the peepul tree. It was a charmed morning, and here was the still center of the spell.

The boy's first words proved this.

"I saw your deer," he said. "Miranda."

They battered him with questions, and he told them how he had noticed the marks of a pair of deer around the temple.

"Look, they are still clear," he said, and sure enough there were the pointed cloven dents of a large and a smaller deer, confused with each other and with the boy's bare prints, but still plain.

"I followed them until they were lost in the grass,

then picked them up on the path," he said, walking ahead to show them. "Then they disappeared again, and I thought the deer might be drinking at the spring and I crept in very quietly, and there they both were, a male and a female. The male had finished but the female was still drinking."

"As I saw her," breathed Phyllida, "as I knew she was."

"It was a lake you saw her by," Annabelle reminded her, but they both wanted to hear the rest of the story and could not stop to argue.

"The male deer heard the crackle of my feet, though I was very quiet," said the boy. "He stamped his hoofs and leaped off. But the female paused for a moment and I spoke to her. I said, 'Hullo Miranda, good morning sister deer'; and she stood there with her ears pointed forward. I thought she was going to come to me. She tossed her head and gave a little squeak, and looked into the jungle, and looked back at me, and then off she went after the male."

"Did you notice anything about her?" Phyllida asked tensely. "About her head?"

The boy pondered a moment.

"There was something about her ears . . . one of her ears had a piece out of it, as if someone had taken a bite at it."

Phyllida nearly cried with relief.

"It was Miranda," she squeaked. "She's had that piece out of her ear ever since we had her. Oh, I'm so glad, so glad. She's safe and happy, and I expect she'll come and see us in our sanctuary."

"She's sure to," said the boy.

"Did you tell her to?" demanded Annabelle, as they walked back to where the tortoise was still standing in the same place swiveling its head from side to side. "You talk deer language, don't you?"

"I can talk to all the animals," said the boy. "I told her to come back."

When they had visited the image and Phyllida had swept out the temple with her bamboo brush—for surprisingly it grew dusty and littered with moth wings and leaves—they sat on the grass around the tortoise and planned. First they would make the pond and clean and scrub the tiles properly. Then they would cut the grass in the glade and perhaps with bamboo stems bring the spring water into it. Later they would plant marigolds.

They set to work on the spring straight away. The boy had brought a small hoe and he scraped out the mud and piled it up for Phyllida and Annabelle to clear away. They carried the tortoise to the spring and set it down in the grass so that they could see it.

"Tell it in tortoise language not to run away," said Annabelle, but the thought of the tortoise running anywhere made them giggle. Its leg seemed better and the boy said it had eaten the leaves he had given it during the night.

Before they had worked for five minutes, it seemed, an hour had gone by and it was time for them to go back for breakfast. The boy had brought his food wrapped in a leaf: two large, thin, grain pancakes, some vegetable curry and a banana. It looked squashed and delicious and they wished they did not have to hurry home to eggs, bacon, table napkins, and school. The knowledge of Miranda and her closeness comforted them and they ran down the path to their ponies cheerfully.

Ginger and Snowball were standing where they had left them, heads hanging, switching at flies.

"Gosh, it's going to be a sizzling day," said Phyllida as they mounted and urged the hot little horses into protesting trots. "It's not eight yet and I'm pouring with sweat."

"So are the ponies," said Annabelle. "We won't ride them again while it's so hot."

They rubbed the horses down and gave them fresh grass when they got in. It was strange not to have Ayah there to put their own heads under the shower and to complain of the mud on their clothes. They missed her knitting figure, but on the whole they were glad she was on the bus and heading for the hills and her home. They galloped upstairs to wash with their thoughts on the afternoon when they could return to the temple glade.

When the afternoon came it was so hot that Annabelle could hardly drag her head from the pillow. As they crossed the lawn the sun was like sword blades on their backs, and their hill monster lay gray and panting, its fur of trees flat on its sullen back. As they walked through the jungle to the temple the air was like warm soapy water. They were reminded of a picture they had seen of a green sulfurous sea with hissing steam rising from it. They made swimming movements with their arms, which made them hotter than ever.

The glade was shaded and peaceful, and the spring water on their faces refreshed them. The boy had not noticed the heat, it seemed. He had dug a pond four feet square and two feet deep around the spring, and banked it strongly, laying a hollow bamboo stem to carry away extra water. He had also cleared a path to the pond, laying the feathery heads of bamboos along it so that they could walk comfortably.

"Us and Miranda," said Phyllida, running on pointed toes like a deer.

They lay on the edge of the pond with their wrists in the water and told the boy how pleased they were with all he had done.

"While we were doing Henry III," Phyllida groaned.

"Ug," said Annabelle, "I hate all those Henrys."

A delightful but wicked thought entered their heads—that one of their mother's aunts might also get ill, and she would have to take herself and the schoolbooks to the aunt's bedside. It was too much to expect, though. Even the boy's grandmother with her magic spells would not be able to make an aunt in England so ill that their mother would leave them and fly to her side. She did not much care for her aunts in any case.

They drew their hands from the water and made plans for the afternoon. They would concentrate on the temple and its round dirty base. They would get it completely free of weeds and moss and tomorrow they would bring scrubbing brushes and their earthen pots and have it glistening. The boy was making a cage for the next animal he found, and busied himself with that. Crickets churred but the birds were silent, resting from the midday heat.

They squatted and scraped, talking rather jerkily. They were all so absorbed that they did not notice that even the crickets had become quiet and it had grown suddenly dark. The first sign they had of the storm was a flash and a crash just above their heads.

"Help!" said Phyllida, and almost as soon as she

had said it a wall of rain fell on them from the sky. They plunged into the temple.

"The tortoise!" Annabelle gasped, but the tortoise was already in the temple sleeping off his exhausting morning. The boy had some matches and they lit the butter lamps and sat in the flickering light beside him, breathing in the good smell of wet stone and wet earth. Phyllida did not care for storms, but here in the glow of the butter lamps and under the smile of the image they felt nothing could harm them.

When it grew calmer and the rain was only a steady gush and the lightning a playful flicker, they went to the door and looked out.

"My grandmother says that the lightning is the daughter of a hill man," the boy said. "She married the god of the sky but when she is homesick he allows her to visit the earth again."

"Well, she's certainly homesick today," said Annabelle, for lightning continued to flicker though the rain had nearly stopped.

"She was running away from a bhoot," the boy added. "The god of the sky rescued her."

Phyllida, who had learned about thunder and lightning in Science, nearly told the boy what she knew, and then decided not to. She looked out into the glade, which was turning from gray to green.

"Are there really bhoots?" she asked the boy.

"Of course."

"Here?"

"Everywhere. Sometimes they are disguised as people. Sometimes as crows or vultures." He pointed at a small silver chain he wore around his neck with a seed at the end of it. "I wear this to protect me against them."

Phyllida looked thoughtful and Annabelle sat in silence. At last Phyllida said, "Could you get me one of those seeds?"

"And me," murmured Annabelle.

"Of course we'll be safe here with the blue god," said Phyllida. Since she had found that the boy and the god shared the same name she had been shy of using it.

"Of course," said Annabelle.

"Bhoots are foolish creatures," said the boy. "You can always get away from them. You just have to know the right words."

"Could you tell us some words?" asked Phyllida casually.

"There are different words for different bhoots," said the boy. "My grandmother knows them all, but I forget. There are so many kinds—tail-snatchers, and head-twisters and blood-suckers. There are different words for each of them."

"And toe-chewers," said Phyllida, "and the ones that live in the graves of the old kings." Bird God

Hill had been the city of some Assamese kings who were buried in mounds all over the tea plantation. Ayah said there was gold in the graves, but also fierce spirits to guard it.

"And those," the boy shrugged. "I do not care about any of them. See, the rain has stopped."

They stepped out into a sodden world, much cooler than the one they had fled from into the temple. Phyllida looked at her watch.

"Nearly five," she gasped. "Help, we must fly." They said good-by to the boy, who promised to shut up and feed the tortoise; and started at a run down the path for home.

"Silly old bhoots," said Phyllida loudly.

"H'm, h'm, h'm," whinnied Annabelle, tossing her head and trying to make flecks of foam at the corners of her mouth. Then with one movement they drew up and stared wide-eyed ahead.

Something was coming along the jungle path toward them. They could hear its feet and the whistling sound of its breath. The grass ahead rustled, but they could see nothing.

"If only we had the seeds," breathed Phyllida.

"Or knew the words," Annabelle hissed.

They turned and started to run back the way they had come. Annabelle was ahead and Phyllida, following her, tripped and fell. At the same moment the thing was on top of her; something brown, something with claws, something slippery and slobbering. She let out a muffled screech and closed her eyes. It was only a peal of laughter from Annabelle that made her open them.

Candy was standing on her back and licking her ears, making the little moaning sounds she always made when she was both happy and worried.

"Candy!" Phyllida exploded. "You nearly made me die of fright."

They sat on the path giggling with relief, and then Annabelle said, "Gosh, the storm must have frightened her. You know how she hates thunder. She must have broken out of the bedroom."

"Poor Candy," cooed Phyllida. "We'll take you with us in the future."

Then another thought occurred to them. Their mother might also have been worried at the storm and gone to see if they were frightened. What excuse could they give for being away from home on such an afternoon?

When they reached the bungalow, they crept upstairs and into their bedroom. The tea tray was under the fan, with the net cover with blue beads over the sandwiches. They sighed with relief. Their mother must have been asleep, as she often was in the afternoon, and missed the storm. They gave Candy three sandwiches before they sat down to eat the rest and laugh about the bhoots.

eight

The Sanctuary Spreads

NEXT MORNING the boy had another basket with a lid on.

"A bird," he said. "Blown out of its nest by the storm."

They peered into the golden eyes of a baby owl.

"How sweet," said Phyllida and put her hand into the basket, and took it out again with a scream. The sweet little owl had raised a clawed foot and raked the palm of her hand, leaving three long bleeding scratches. The boy bound her hand with one of the leaves he always carried in his pocket.

"We will have to leave it in the basket for a few days," he said. "When we have fed it a little it will let us handle it."

They stared at the owl, and it hissed at them, hatred bristling from every feather. Peering through the cracks they saw it was fully fledged, with gaiters of downy white hair and a white ruff which rose around its neck every time they looked at it.

"It's a screech owl," said Phyllida. "It'll eat lizards and mice and things."

"Its mother chews these things up for it and drops them into its mouth with the skin on," said the boy.

None of them liked the idea of chewing lizards, and they sat for a moment in silence, considering its feeding.

"Probably owl spit is different from ours," said Phyllida at last. "Probably our spit would poison it."

"My spit would," said Annabelle firmly.

"We will have to give it meat," said the boy. "We can dip it into water to soften it. Later it can eat small lizards whole."

So when they returned in the afternoon they brought a chunk of Candy's beef and cut this into little pieces. The boy covered his hand with a rag and lowered it into the owl's basket, a piece of wet meat between his finger and thumb. The owl's eyes blazed and it snapped its beak angrily. It would not touch the meat. When the boy continued to press it to its beak, it turned its head away and closed its eyes.

"We shall have to get the lizards," said Phyllida. "We could grind them up and then spit on them."

"Ug." Annabelle made a noise as if she were going to be sick.

"Worms," suggested the boy. But the owl did not want worms, or beetles, or caterpillars, or a grasshopper. Each time they offered it one of these things it looked more offended and swiveled its neck around so that the back of its head was facing them.

"We shall have to force it to eat," said the boy. "Otherwise it will die. I will hold its legs and you must open its beak and push a piece of meat down."

There was a flapping and hissing and clattering of the owl's beak, and then he had it out of the basket, its taloned gaitered legs firmly held with one hand, its wings with the other. Phyllida gingerly approached its beak, grasped it at the base, and pushed a piece of meat in. The owl snapped its beak on the meat but made no attempt to swallow it. It sat there glowering at them, with the meat clamped in between the two curves of its beak. They watched it and made swallowing noises hopefully.

"It looks like an old man smoking a pipe," said Annabelle. "What shall we do now?"

"We shall have to push it down," said Phyllida, suddenly remembering the babyhood of Herbert and other birds they had kept. "Mother birds always push it right down the back of their babies' throats."

The boy tightened his hold on the owl's wings,

and Phyllida grasped its head again from the back and forced open the clenched beak. Then very bravely she put her finger inside the owl's mouth and pushed the meat as far as she could down its throat. It gulped, hissed, clattered its beak furiously and scrabbled with its talons, but the meat had gone.

"Another piece," said the boy, and the performance was repeated. The third time, as Phyllida prepared to hold its head, it leaned forward, took the meat from her hand, shook it, and swallowed it. They stared at it in amazement and then at each other, and then burst out laughing in relief. The owl squinted and gave a distinct hiccup.

They decided to give it one more piece, just to see if it had not been a fluke, and this time the owl positively grabbed the meat.

"We will not give it any more for now," said the boy. "We will feed it often but a little at a time, and then it will get used to the new food."

"You could talk to it in owl language and tell it we're trying to help," said Annabelle. She did not believe the boy could speak the languages he claimed, and was always trying to make him prove it.

"I will tell it now," said the boy, and he leaned around and looked into the owl's unblinking eyes. He made soft cooing noises, quite unlike its own. Then he straightened and very gently released the fluffy white legs he held so firmly imprisoned. He lowered the yellow, razor-sharp feet onto his free hand.

The owl was standing, swaying slightly, on the back of his hand. The knife claws hardly made dents in his skin. It clattered its beak, but gently, and its thoughts were obviously turned inward to the meat that was lying in its stomach. For a long moment they watched it, hardly daring to breathe. Then the boy picked it up casually around its plump waist and put it back in its basket.

They thought the boy wonderful and told him so.

"Oh," he said shrugging, but pleased, "it only pretends to be fierce. My grandmother says it got the orange fire in its eyes from the tiger. There was an argument—oh, many years ago—about the day and the night. Men wanted it to be always day, and the tiger wanted it to be always night. So they had a meeting and the owl was appointed as judge. The owl decided that it should be half day and half night, and the tiger was so angry that he cuffed it over the head. The flame of his own anger went into the owl's eyes, and his paw flattened the owl's head. But the gods agreed with the owl, they too thought there should be half day and half night in the world."

"Haven't we got a clever pair of animals," said Phyllida. "Both cleverer than the tiger."

She looked at the tortoise, which was walking slowly across the glade, dragging one leg slightly. Candy, who had come with them, fled from the tortoise, but Candy was a coward. Somehow a limping tortoise and a small hiccuping owl hardly seemed like tiger scarers.

Nor, to be quite honest, when she had thought of a sanctuary had she peopled it with ceatures like these. Still they had to start somewhere, and the blue god was not fussy. These were his care, just as were the elephants and black panthers which would undoubtedly follow.

"We must give them names," she said. "What about White Legs for the owl?"

"Or Yellow Feet," said Annabelle scornfully, "or Brown Back for the tortoise."

"Well, you think of names then," Phyllida snapped, "since you're so clever."

Annabelle thought for a moment.

"We could call the tortoise Pegasus," she suggested.

"Honestly!" Phyllida exploded. "You and your horses. It's not like Pegasus in one single way."

"It's got four legs."

Phyllida looked around for something to throw, and the boy said, "Why not just Lengra—the lame one."

They thought about this and because nobody

could think of a better name they decided to call the tortoise Lengra. Then there was the owl.

"He reminds me of the period in history when they wore white stockings and ruffs around their necks," said Annabelle. "When was that?"

"Sir Walter Raleigh," said Phyllida, who had read a book about him and remembered the ruff distinctly.

So the owl became Sir Walter, which the boy found hard to say, and they called him Walt.

For a week after the naming nothing new happened in the glade. They brought brushes and scrubbed out the temple. The owl ate voraciously and the boy made him a big cage which they hung on the peepul tree. Miranda did not return but they saw deer prints by the spring and were happy about her. Under their hands the glade was transformed. The boy chopped the long grass and weeds with his square knife so that the temple sat serenely on a clean green mound.

They swept the leaves under the peepul tree and the boy began a still bigger cage, taking in a couple of branches of the tree, so that the owl would have freedom to use his wings as soon as they were ready. They planned to put Lengra the tortoise in with him. In spite of his injured leg Lengra was beginning to wander out of the glade, and they did not think he was ready to take up his life as tiger-frightener just yet.

The boy changed the jungle for them. They had thought of it as a collection of leaves and grasses with no particular purpose except to harbor wild animals and bhoots. He moved through it whistling, as a boy would walk through a town, searching for what he needed: string, a catapult, a fishing basket, soap, pen, and ink. All these things the jungle provided, either ready-made like the nuts that lathered for soap or the bark that cleaned his teeth; or waiting for his knife to work on, like the different bamboos which he shaped, wove, bound, and curled into anything he wanted.

If it was wet there were the huge leaves of the palmetto ferns for umbrellas; if dry, the smaller ones for fans. The wild bananas would make him a shelter for the night. Stones held fire, and any patch of water, fish, which he could coax out with a berry on a strong sharp thorn. As he collected bamboos he also picked the herbs his grandmother needed, and curly ferns for their curry, and dug up roots. He knew which plants stung, and which cured stings, and how to keep off leeches and mosquitoes.

They did not move far from the glade, but seeing it with his eyes it became a vast, newly discovered country. He showed them where an animal had lain in the night—it was a civet cat, here was one of its hairs—and the scratch marks of a bigger cat on the bark of a tree, a leopard he thought. Deer liked this, wild pig rooted for that, bees would come later to this tree, and look, there was the old eavesdropper, the bulbul. He was the messenger of the animal world, and would fly around to report to them all the doings of man in their jungle.

He had a story for everything: for the calls of the birds, for their colors and shapes, for the reason why there was only one sun in the sky and why the frog had lumps on its back and why the crab's eyes popped out.

"Do you believe him?" Annabelle asked in English after he had described how the python spat out its poison because nobody liked it, and how the bees and the smaller snakes picked it up.

"I don't know," said Phyllida, also in English. To the boy they talked the language they spoke to the servants. "It doesn't seem to matter, really."

Believing or not believing seemed the same thing in the glade. Sometimes when she was there Phyllida felt so close to the earth and the plants and the animals that she was surprised that her own legs were not furred or her arms feathered. In the jungle Annabelle became a wild horse and discarded her rubber bit. She tore around on her unshod hoofs neighing the wild happiness of all the world's unsaddled stallions.

It was the morning of the eighth day since they had found the owl, and Phyllida sat scratching her ankles. She had forgotten to rub her legs with the plant the boy had given her and two leeches had fastened on her as she walked to the temple. The boy was working on the big cage for Walt, which he had nearly finished. He would cut thatch for its roof, he said, to protect the animals from sun and rain. He came to crouch beside Phyllida, whittling as always at a piece of bamboo. Annabelle had given her wild horse two gallops around the glade and came to throw herself in the grass between them, lying on her side and blowing her stomach in and out like a panting stallion.

"Oh, my *legs*," said Phyllida, tearing at her ankles. It was an overcast morning and mosquitoes were adding to the itches of the leech bites.

"Here," said the boy, and handed her the leaf whose juice would keep off these pests. "You should carry these always. My grandmother says leeches and mosquitoes are really a bhoot."

"Gosh, another kind," said Annabelle. "I thought we knew them all."

"A bhoot called Aboo Toontotoonga," continued the boy. "He chased two village boys up a tree, and they threw their swords down and told him to make a ladder of them. Of course he cut his feet trying to climb a sword ladder, and then they hid under a bridge and chopped it down as he was crossing it. He was drowned, but his wife was so angry that she

*109

ground his body up into little pieces on a flat stone, and each one turned into a mosquito or a leech; and she told them to suck men's blood as a revenge."

"Most of the revenge seems to be on me," said Phyllida. "Go away, Aboo Toontotoonga," she shouted at a mosquito. "I didn't kill you, you silly old bhoot."

"Bhoots are *terribly* silly," said Annabelle. "I'm not the least scared of them."

Most of their morning had gone, and Phyllida went off to pick leaves for Lengra. She went to the spring first to see if there were new prints, but there were none.

"She will come, I know she will," she said.

She dipped her forehead in the water and then sauntered a short way down the path out of the glade.

"We are making these paths too plain," she decided. "We must use new ones."

She thought of the wife of Aboo Toontotoonga grinding his body on a flat stone, the way the cook ground spices for curry, and she rounded a corner to see an old woman sitting at the bottom of a tree grinding something on a large stone. She let out a shriek and fled.

"A bhoot," she bellowed to Annabelle and the boy, "a lady one."

"Where?" asked the boy.

"Help!" squeaked Annabelle. "Did you have your seed?"

Phyllida had forgotten about the seed she carried in her pocket as a protection against bhoots. She was breathless as she explained to them how terrible the old woman had looked.

"She had turned-up yellow eyes like a cat's," she gasped. "And pointed fangs. And she was grinding up bones."

"Let us go and see her," said the boy.

"Do you know the words?" Annabelle asked anxiously, "for ladies I mean."

"I know lots of words," he said calmly. "I will try them all."

"Gosh, I hope they work quickly," said Phyllida. "She might have turned us all into toads by the time you get to the right ones."

The boy took his square knife in his hand and led the way down the path. Candy went next, and when she got to the corner she stopped and the hair stood up all the way down her spine. The boy, who had peered around, his knife ready, suddenly threw back his head and hooted with laughter.

"What is it?" hissed Phyllida. "What's so funny?"

"Ai-ee," hooted the boy, and he had to sit down and drop his head between his knees. "Grinding up bones," he hiccuped. "Ai-ee. Ai-ee."

*111

"For heaven's sake," said Annabelle, peeking and seeing what Phyllida had seen, and drawing back quickly. "What's so funny?"

"That is not a bhoot," sniffed the boy. "That is my grandmother."

nine

A Riddle

PHYLLIDA had rarely felt like such a fool. She apologized to the boy, but neither he nor his grandmother seemed the least annoyed. The boy went closer and bellowed into the old woman's ear that they had thought she was a bhoot and she cackled even louder and longer than he had done. They saw that she was in fact grinding areca nuts, not bones.

"Gosh, I'm sorry," said Phyllida several times, but the boy said it was a mistake anyone could make. And they all trailed back to the temple in silence, except the grandmother who was still cackling.

Now that they came to look at her closely she was rather beautiful. She had skin the color of old silk, and her tilted eyes were only one shade darker than gold. Her hair was paper white and drawn tightly back from her forehead. She wore a great coiled snake of silver around her throat and several smaller snakes on her arms; and a shower of blue and red

*113

stones hung from her ears, which were pulled almost to her shoulders with the weight.

In spite of her white hair and the wrinkles that ran across her skin like creases in silk, she was a very active old lady. She skipped about the temple glade, making loud exclamations in front of Walt and Lengra, tweaking the children's noses, shouting at the image and the carvings, and finally standing in the center of the glade with her own head between her hands, whooping with approval.

"So beautiful, so beautiful!" she cried. "Aha, aha, how beautiful you have made it!"

Then she rounded on Phyllida and Annabelle, pressed them in a suffocating embrace, and did a sort of dance with them around the temple. When she released them Phyllida said in a breathless voice, "I'm afraid we must go now. It's time for breakfast."

"They have to go," shouted the boy. "My grandmother is deaf," he explained rather unnecessarily.

The old lady hugged them again, her silver bracelets cutting into her arms, and they raced back to the paddock and jumped on to their ponies in a daze.

"Gosh," Phyllida said. "What a funny sort of grandmother. She's not a bit like a witch, though, is she."

"More like a python the way she squeezed," said Annabelle.

They rather hoped the grandmother would not be there when they returned in the afternoon; but she was, and so was a real python. It was tied by a rope lead to the trunk of the peepul tree. It was the biggest snake they had ever seen.

"We dragged it between us," said the boy. "It took us a long time. Now we have a proper animal, no?"

"But is it hurt?" asked Phyllida, eyeing the python from a safe distance.

"It is sick," the boy said. "Its stomach hurts. Otherwise we could not have caught it. We will look after it."

The python did look sick, and very sad. It lay in a sullen coil and only raised its head at intervals to give a small hiss. It had a mouth as big as a cow's, and large teeth.

The grandmother stroked its tail and cackled delightedly, and this the python did not seem to mind.

"A real animal, heh?" she demanded. "Ah, you wait, my darlings. I will bring you a dozen of these."

"I think one will do," said Annabelle in a small voice, but the grandmother did not hear.

"And others," she croaked. "Tigers and bears and wild red dogs. I will fill this place with animals."

"Thank you very much," said Phyllida. "But what are we going to give this one to eat? And where will we put it?"

"Frogs and lizards," said the boy. "It will eat almost anything."

"It'll eat Lengra." Phyllida suddenly had an even more horrible thought. "It'll eat Miranda if she comes here."

In fact the python would not eat anything. They found several frogs and dropped them in front of it, turning away their heads and blocking their ears so that they would not hear the crunch; but the frogs hopped out of the way and the python did not even watch them go.

"It has just eaten," said the boy. "It will not want to eat again for a few days."

"Silly creature," said the grandmother, going very close and shaking a finger at it. She looked for a moment as if she were going to hug it. Instead, to their horror, she sat down and ran a finger over its head and down its back.

"Such beautiful skin," she crooned. "I could use that skin. I could mix it with the blood of an owl and the feather of a peacock and the milk of a cow with a black and white calf. Ai-ee, such medicine I could make."

The python seemed to like the feel of her finger

down its spine, but Phyllida and Annabelle felt shivers down theirs.

"You have explained to your grandmother that this is a sanctuary, haven't you?" Phyllida questioned the boy urgently.

"Ah, she is only joking," the boy said. "She uses herbs for her medicines. She would not use the blood of your owl in any case."

"I should hope *not*," said Annabelle.

The grandmother continued to croon over the python while they discussed the best place to put it. The inside of the temple seemed the only safe spot. It was too fat to get out through the cracks in the windows. But where was Lengra to go, and Walt? There was no telling when the python's appetite would return.

"We shall have to take them back to our house at night," said the boy, and they had to agree. The next problem was to get the python into the temple.

"We will bind its mouth," said the boy casually. "As we did when we brought it here." And he deftly wound a piece of strong bamboo around the large head and drew it tight, holding the jaws together. The python, who seemed to have been hypnotized by the grandmother's fingers, made no protest, and allowed them to carry and haul it across the grass to the temple, and push it inside. When they had the door shut they cut the rope from its neck and jaws. It lay where they had put it, under the alcove where the carved figure with the umbrella sat. It seemed to take up half the temple.

"It is only a small one," the boy apologized.

"It's quite big enough," Phyllida assured him. "When its appetite comes back we shall be frog hunting all day."

She wished the python looked happier. Soon it would, she felt sure, once it knew where it was and under whose protection. She had no time to worry about its feelings for long, because the grandmother grasped her arm and Annabelle's and dragged both of them out into the sunshine and up to the peepul tree. She pushed them down, sat between them, and opened the cloth bag at her waist.

"For you my darlings," she shouted, handing them each a round ball, warm and crumbly. "Eat it," she commanded, grinding her own jaws fiercely. "Why aren't you eating it? EAT IT."

They took a nibble at the ball. It tasted quite unlike anything they had eaten before.

"I hope it's not owl's blood," murmured Annabelle.

"What did you say?" demanded the grandmother. "You don't like it?"

"Oh yes, very much, thank you," Phyllida said, drawing back her lips and dislodging a tiny crumb from the side of the ball and chewing on this heartily. Annabelle, she noticed, had managed to drop most of hers, and then edge over and sit on it.

"My grandson must stay at home to plant our rice next week," the grandmother told them. "That is why I have come. Are you glad I have come?"

"Yes, very glad." Phyllida was still munching the same crumb and the thought of a week with the grandmother and the python made her nearly choke on it.

"We shall have to plant our own rice," Annabelle announced.

"Mice?" said the grandmother. "Baba, I will bring you a black panther next."

"RICE," Annabelle bellowed. "We are going to plant it too," and she made scratching signs and put her finger and thumb into an imaginary hole in the ground. The grandmother pounced on her and pushed her head down.

"They said rice," said the boy, "not lice."

The grandmother let go of Annabelle's head and rocked backward and forward, shrieking with laughter at her mistake in thinking that Annabelle wanted the lice taken from her hair. The colored stones in her ears jingled and glittered.

"My ears," she shouted, pulling at the huge weighted lobes. "They are like the ears of the elephant when the bat flew into them."

In fact they did look a lot like elephant's ears, but before they had time to decide whether to agree with her, she had leaned forward and grasped one of Phyllida's ears.

"Like a cowrie shell," she exclaimed. "Like a lotus. So white and smooth. So beautiful." It was the same crooning voice she had used when she had been stroking the python. Phyllida drew away her ear as politely as she could.

"They're not white really," she said, edging away and managing to sit on the hand in which she held the crumbled remains of the brown ball. "They're jolly dirty. Black in fact."

This remark sent the grandmother into hysterics. She rolled about, holding her head between her palms; but they did not know what she imagined Phyllida had said and could only smile politely. At last she stopped laughing, wiped her yellow eyes on the corner of the cloth she wore over her shoulders, and drew them to her in a tremendous, tight embrace.

"You want to know the secret of this place?" she yelled. "My grandson tells me you want to know."

"Yes, *please*," Phyllida yelled back breathlessly.

"There are no keys," said the grandmother. "No locks. No doors or windows."

"Please tell us the secret," shouted Annabelle desperately. "We won't breathe a word."

*121

"No word," said the grandmother. "No spell, or medicine. Only I have it here," and she tapped her head with her knuckles.

"Tell them the riddle," said the boy, coming up to help the conversation. "At least tell them that." Although he did not shout she seemed to hear him perfectly.

"Ai-ee, the riddle." She rocked back and forth, taking them with her as she still held them by the shoulders. "Ai-ee, they will never solve that. Never."

"Tell us," pleaded Phyllida. "We can try."

"And if you find out the secret?" she demanded, suddenly looking very fierce. "What then?"

"Nothing," Phyllida assured her.

"Then why do you want to know?" asked the grandmother, who seemed able to hear when she needed to.

"We don't want to know," said Annabelle, freeing herself from the encircling arm with its hard bracelets. "We have plenty of secrets of our own, you can keep yours," and kicking up her heels she galloped off, whinnying in her most carefree manner.

This seemed to have just the right effect.

"Come back, my darling," screeched the grandmother. "Come back, my sweetie. I will tell you the riddle."

Annabelle sidled up, tossing her head and rolling

suspicious eyes. She shied away from the grand-mother's efforts to catch hold of her again, and stood wheezing and pawing the ground just out of reach. Phyllida, who wished she had thought of this scheme, said, "Don't go on and on. If you make her angry she'll never tell us."

"Who cares?" said Annabelle, but they both did care, and watched the grandmother anxiously.

She carried a cloth bag at her waist as Ayah did, and out of this she now drew some pieces of stick which she arranged on the ground in front of her in a pattern. Then round them she drew in the mud a square box.

"You see?" said the boy. "It means nothing."

Phyllida and Annabelle squatted near the pattern and stared at it.

"That's the riddle?" asked Phyllida.

"That is part of it," said the boy. "The other part means nothing either. Tell them," he commanded his grandmother.

And she began to sing in a high singsong voice:

"What is deeper than root of the tal-sal tree?
What is darker than porcupine's burrow?
Seek a white stone, seek a white stone,
Will spiders' eggs bring you sorrow?"

"You see," said the boy again.

"Could you say it once more, please?" asked Phyllida.

"Again," the boy said in the old woman's ear;
once more she droned the riddle.

"Thank you," Phyllida said. "I think I've got it
now," and she pursed her lips and shook her head in
a very wise way.

"You know what it means?" cried the grandmother.

"Not yet," said Phyllida, "but I will," and she
nodded her head again very solemnly.

"You look like Walt wanting his meat," said
Annabelle, "bobbing up and down like that," and she
imitated the way Phyllida was nodding.

"You look like the python, all fat and sluggish,"
said Phyllida, sticking out her stomach. But they
only said these things to show they were not worried
about solving the riddle.

Talking of Walt and the python reminded Phyllida to look at her watch, and then it was a race to
feed the hungry little owl, check up on the snake,
and make plans for the next few days when they
would all be busy with their rice. The grandmother

said she would come and spend the day at the temple while the boy worked. She would also arrange for lots of new animals, she said.

Phyllida and Annabelle would come for short periods bringing the meat for Walt, and helping with the frog catching. Both the owl and the tortoise were to be taken home by the boy and his grandmother, and they closed the temple door firmly on the python, who was lying in the same sulky lump as before.

Lying in bed that night they talked about the grandmother and her riddle.

"I think she's terrible," said Annabelle. "I hope she doesn't stay long."

"She is rather awful," Phyllida agreed, "but she does know stories about animals, and the secret."

"What secret?" said Annabelle as scornfully as she could with her eyes closing. "I don't believe there's a secret."

"I do," said Phyllida.

She repeated the riddle in the singsong voice the grandmother had used. Somewhere in the back of her head a memory was lurking, but what it was and what connection it had with the riddle she was too sleepy to decide. Her last thought was of the python asleep in the temple.

"Please take care of him," she prayed, but whether to her own or to the blue god she was not sure.

*125

ten

A Stone and a Clue

THEY CREPT into the glade next morning and looked
around. It was empty.

"Cheers," said Phyllida. "She's not here."

Then they saw that the temple door was open, and
Candy, with her nose to the ground, was pressing
against their legs and shivering.

"She's here all right," said Annabelle, and very
slowly they walked over and stood in the door. An
extraordinary sight met their eyes.

The grandmother was sitting on the python, and
on the grandmother's shoulder, his yellow eyes on a
line with her own, was Walt. They all three seemed
happy and at home together, and the image beamed
his approval.

"Good morning my darlings," yelled the grandmother. "Have you solved the riddle yet? Eh?"
and she leaped up and skipped across to embrace

them. Walt teetered but kept his balance, and the python continued to lie still.

"Not yet," said Phyllida, disentangling herself once more from the bracelets and the earrings. "Here, I've got your meat, Walt."

She was jealous that the little owl, who had always refused her own arm or shoulder, should have settled so confidently on a strange one. Walt took the piece of meat she offered, but when she tried to pick him up, he raised his ruff and clattered his beak angrily.

They all went out into the glade and Annabelle muttered, "She's cast a spell on him. She'll be taking his blood next."

"Come, Walt," cooed Phyllida, and dangled a piece of meat just out of his reach. He leaned forward, and as his balance became unsteady Phyllida grabbed him. In a flash one of his taloned feet had clawed the back of her arm.

"Ow!" she shrieked.

"I told you so," shouted Annabelle.

"Blood!" yelled the grandmother. She drew out of her bag one of the leaves the boy carried and pressed it to the scratches, wrapping the arm in an old shred of cloth from the same bag. Walt flapped his wings, and looked into the distance. "You wicked owl," the grandmother bellowed, shaking a finger at him. "You poor darling," she said in the same voice to Phyllida. "All that lovely blood wasting. Come, I have something for you that will make you forget."

She scrabbled in her bag once more and brought out some lumps of bright green jelly.

"Eat it," she commanded in the way she had done for the brown balls. "And you, EAT IT," and she pushed a lump into Annabelle's mouth.

It had the same taste, neither sour nor sweet, nice nor nasty, as the balls had had. Phyllida took a tiny nibble, but Annabelle did a quick gallop around the glade and spat hers into the grass. She saw it land in a glutinous glob, and on the next round noticed that it was already covered with ants.

"Don't swallow any," she hissed to Phyllida as she cantered past. "It's a spell, like she's cast on Walt."

Phyllida rolled the bit of jelly around and around in her mouth and became rather flushed. The grandmother was watching her, and soon she would have to take another bite. Luckily their eyes were drawn to Annabelle when she screamed.

"The python!" She pointed to the temple. "Look!"

They turned to see a gray stream of snake slowly pouring out of the temple door. The python looked around vaguely and then eased itself over to the peepul tree and very slowly drifted up. Its great soft body slid up the trunk of the tree as if it were a paper snake pulled on some gigantic string. It rolled along a branch, and then laid its head down and sighed, and slept.

"Gosh," said Phyllida. "Now what are we going to do?"

"We'll have to lasso it," said Annabelle. "But not me," she added hastily.

"Not to worry, not to worry," laughed the grandmother. "He likes it there. Let him stay. He will find birds to eat, and rats and lizards."

"He might drop on us one day when he's hungry," Phyllida said, remembering a picture of a man in the coils of a giant snake which was slowly crushing him. "Or Candy." She picked up the trembling dog and held her close.

"I won't feel very happy with him just lying there waiting to pounce," said Annabelle. "Perhaps he'll go away in the night."

"Bite? He will never bite," the grandmother said. "He may be a god in disguise, my darlings. There were many gods who took the shape of snakes. There was a village boy too who lived in a python's skin. He lived in a hole at the bottom of a tree. One day a girl came and sheltered from the rain in his hole. She was the most beautiful girl in the world, as beautiful as a white stone, and she married him."

"A hole in the bottom of a tree," repeated Phyllida. "A white stone. But that sounds like. . . ."

"Well, my darlings, I have work to do," shouted the grandmother, leaping to her feet in a flash of silver, blue, and red. "Am I to sit here all day staring at sleeping snakes? I must make medicine and help my grandson with the rice."

"Will you rub the medicine in first thing in the morning?" said Phyllida.

"Eh?"

"The medicine? Will you rub it into the snake?"

"Cake? I will bring you cake tomorrow. Now I have only these. Here you are, my darling, and you." And the grandmother thrust some more of the green lumps into their hands and with a last affectionate grab and shake at their ears she was gone, with Walt on her shoulder.

"It's jolly peculiar," said Phyllida thoughtfully.

"What is?" asked Annabelle. "Her?"

"The hole at the foot of the tree and the girl like a white stone. It sounds just like the riddle. 'What is deeper than root of the tal-sal tree, what is darker than porcupine's burrow, seek a white stone, seek a white stone. . . .' "

"A hole at the foot of a tal-sal tree with a white stone near it," said Annabelle, excited in spite of herself. "That's all we've got to find."

"And some spiders' eggs," Phyllida reminded her.

"Do you happen to know what spiders' eggs look like?"

"No. Do you know what a tal-sal tree looks like?"

"No."

They sighed, their eyes on the sleeping python.

"But there's the white stone," said Annabelle. "We could look for that first."

They slid their eyes from the snake and stared around the glade. The stones of the temple were pink except the windows which were gray.

"Let's look inside," said Phyllida. "I know I've seen a white stone somewhere."

With their eyes on the python they edged carefully toward the temple, and stepped inside. The sun was sending a first beam through one of the windows, and it lay on the floor like a finger pointing at the image. The god was white in the early light, and so was the stone on which he sat.

"A white stone," breathed Phyllida.

"Grayish," said Annabelle. "It only looks white now because of the sun."

"That might be part of the trick. Come on, let's see if it's loose."

Gently they lifted the image and put it in another niche. Then with beating hearts they pulled at the stone beneath.

"It's loose," hissed Phyllida. "I knew it. The secret's underneath."

*131

"But what about the porcupine's burrow and. . . ."

"Help pull," said Phyllida impatiently. "There may be a message or something to tell us about that."

The large square stone wobbled as they tugged at it, but they could not get it free. Phyllida took her penknife off its chain and dug at the cracks between the stone and the wall. This seemed to loosen the stone a little more, but not enough to lift it out.

"Let's ask the image to help," said Annabelle. "You ask him, you believe in him."

Phyllida looked at the little white figure smiling from his new niche, and shook her head.

"We can't bother him with things like this," she said. "Otherwise when we're really in trouble he won't believe us. I know, what about the grandmother's jelly? It might have some sort of spell in it."

They pulled out the green lumps the grandmother had given them before she left.

"We can sort of smear them around the cracks," said Phyllida, and she began to rub her bit of jelly energetically up and down.

"I think it'll be like glue and stick the stone harder," said Annabelle, but she followed Phyllida's example and scraped the other side of the stone with her lump. After a few seconds there were bits of jelly stuck along the cracks and their knuckles were raw. Candy stood on her hind legs and licked the stone, and Phyllida smacked her.

"Do you want to turn into a toad, you clod?" she scolded. "That's magic jelly."

Candy lay on her back with her four feet waving apologetically and they waited for the magic to work.

"We'll count to ten slowly and then pull again," said Phyllida; but they had only reached seven when they realized that something was happening to the stone. At first it seemed as if the cracks were moving, but as they peered closer they saw it was a stream of ants. They had appeared from under the stone and were collecting in clusters around the lumps of jelly. Annabelle wanted to shoo them away but Phyllida stopped her. It might be part of the spell, she said.

The ants jostled and scrambled, and then parties of them hoisted the sticky green morsels up and started back down the cracks, bumping into all the later excited ants coming in the opposite direction.

"Look, they're going down that hole in the corner," said Phyllida. "They must live under the stone."

"That doesn't help us much."

"Well, it shows there must be a space underneath. Come on, let's try pulling again."

*133

They waved their hands over the ants to warn them, and when they had all scurried away, grasped the stone again. This time, perhaps because the ants had been moving and loosened the earth in the cracks, the stone moved much more easily.

"One, two, three, *heave*," they gasped, and the stone lurched and came free. They let go and fell on top of Candy who yapped and fled. Hardly daring to breathe, they lifted the stone carefully and lowered it to the floor. Then they looked at the place where it had rested.

"Ants," said Annabelle in disgust.

"And eggs," said Phyllida hopefully. "Perhaps they're spider's eggs."

"What would ants be doing with spider's eggs? Don't be silly. It's just an ants' nest with mother and father ants and egg babies."

The ants were dashing about in the hole under the stone carrying their eggs in their mouths, panic-stricken.

"Poor things," said Phyllida. "It must be like the end of the world will be for us."

"Without the trumpets," said Annabelle. "Let's cover them up again and they can eat the green jelly and cheer themselves up."

Phyllida bent down over the hole and squinted into it.

"There's something sort of pink in there," she said. "It looks like . . . ow."

She had put her finger into the hole and several ants had attacked it and were still clinging to the tip as she drew it out. She shook them off, blew on her finger, and then dug her penknife carefully in among them to pry out the pink object she had seen. When she pulled it out she saw it was a small clay pot, round at the bottom, with a long neck. She tipped it upside down and several ants fell out, but there was still something inside which rattled.

"A porcupine probably," said Annabelle in a voice she tried to make sound scornful, but couldn't. "Go on, shake it harder. Break it."

"Certainly not. It's probably terribly old and valuable. We'll probably be famous for finding it." Phyllida shook the pot again and then gently inserted her little finger. There was something round and hard stuck in the neck, and she could not shift it.

"Give it to me," said Annabelle. "My finger's smaller."

But Annabelle's smaller finger could not dislodge the round object from the neck of the pot, and it was not until they found a thin piece of bamboo and gently prodded and twisted for several minutes that they were able to loosen it. While they worked they guessed what would fall out: a very valuable jewel seemed likely, or perhaps a tiny gold box with a key in it which would fit another box which would finally reveal the secret. . . .

When a blackened coin fell into Phyllida's palm they let out a groan of disappointment.

"It's probably terribly old," said Phyllida.

"That makes it even worse; we can't spend it," Annabelle complained. "This isn't a white stone, I knew it wasn't and there aren't any spider's eggs or a porcupine's burrow. . . ."

"Oh, don't go on and on about porcupines," Phyllida snapped. "We've got to try everything. Anyway, this has some writing on it. It might be a message."

She rubbed the coin with her shirt and they were able to see that on one side there was indeed writing; but it was in a script they could not understand, Assamese presumably. On the other side there was the head of a man.

"A king it must be, on a coin," said Phyllida.

"One of the old kings of Assam," said Annabelle.

They tried to see what possible connection this fact had with the grandmother's riddle, but could find none. A yap from Candy brought them back to earth, and they ran out to find her sitting shivering at the foot of the peepul tree, staring up at the still sleeping snake.

"He'll eat you for breakfast, you silly creature," said Phyllida, scooping Candy up and backing away from the tree with her. Then they remembered their own breakfast would be waiting for them, so they had to hurry to replace the stone as carefully as they could on top of the ants, and the image on top of the stone. Phyllida took another long look at the king on her coin before she put it into her pocket.

"It could be a clue," she murmured.

That afternoon it rained and they planted their rice. The malis helped them dig up the lemon-green stalks, and then together they pounded and pulped the wet earth. They let water from the pond into the field to flood it, and settled the clumps of young rice into the sloshy ground in rows. It looked very pretty, but it took a long time. When they had admired the tender tassels of rice reflected in the water they stacked what was left in their little hut. Some they would plant the next day, some they gave to the malis; one clump they kept to place on the temple floor in front of the image.

The sun was turning the rice to gold and the water beneath it to flame when at last they tore themselves away.

"It is byootiful, byootiful, byootiful," Phyllida chanted as they trailed their muddy way back to the bungalow. "As byootiful as a white stone."

"I'm a leech and this is blood I'm oozing," said

*137

Annabelle as she dragged her wet feet along the veranda, leaving a sticky trail behind.

"I'm a bhoot with bleeding feet," said Phyllida. "I'm Aboo Toontotoonga."

In the kitchen they found a letter from Ayah, so with the mud drying on their legs they read it.

"Darling Fillda and Ennebel," it said.

"At first take my loving greet. I am well by the grace of god and hoping you are likewise. My auntie is pulling along somehow, she is lying all day on bed like an old log. She is better. I am bringing hunny and porks and other things. I am returning soon, I do not know when I am returning. Pleas take my loving greet to Memsahib and Daddy-sahib. Now I must say good by.

Your sweet Ayah."

"Darling Ayah," said Phyllida. "I hope auntie stays like an old log a bit longer. About two months."

"Wouldn't she have a fit if she saw us now?" said Annabelle. "H'm, h'm, I dibs the first bath."

"As byootiful as a white stone," crooned Phyllida, swinging her muddy legs. She drew the coin from her pocket and stared at it. "I'm sure it's a clue, I'm sure, I'm sure."

Later she was to remember she had been right. The coin with the king on it was indeed a clue.

eleven

Brindaban Blossoms

THE NEXT few days were much the same: a visit to the glade in the morning with Walt's meat; a fight not to be enchanted by the grandmother's sweets; and rice planting in the afternoon. The python moved farther up the peepul tree and Walt looked as if he were growing out of the grandmother's shoulder.

"Her familiar spirit," said Annabelle grimly. "Witches always have them."

When their rice plot was finished they felt very satisfied. Then the sadness came over them that when they cut it they would be leaving Assam, but that was a long time ahead. Now it was only the beginning of August, and the rice would turn dark green, then pale yellow, then deep burnt gold, and by then they would have solved the riddle.

Herbert came down to the pond and sat looking at the rice with his head on one side, measuring like them how long it would be before it was ready.

They would have to watch that he did not get it before them, he and his hundreds of hungry friends with whom he spent more and more time.

One of these days, they knew, the call of the hills would be too strong and he would join the sweeping crescents of parrots that trailed across every dawn and sunset. They envied him. If they could have had a wish it would have been to be turned into Assamese parrots. Never to leave the Naga hills and the plains beneath them! Never to go to school and wear wool vests and shoes with laces!

They wondered if the grandmother could turn them into parrots, and how much their parents would mind. On the last evening, when they had planted the last rice clump, they were so tired that they crawled upstairs on their hands and knees and very slowly along the passage, dragging their legs like Lengra.

Next day, when they took the rice seedlings to the temple, they found the boy was there, and the grandmother, and each had an animal. The boy was carrying on his hip a little gray ape, and the grandmother was squatting beside an anteater the size of a small crocodile.

"How super!" they shouted, running from one to the other. The ape bared square yellow teeth in a frightened grin and clung closer to the boy, giving thin piercing screams. The anteater hid its long pointed face in its clawed feet. Walt peered down at it from the grandmother's shoulder, his eyes bright with angry tigerfire.

It seemed that the anteater had been attacked, for several inches were missing from the end of its tail. The wound looked recent and raw. The baby ape must have lost its mother, the boy said. The Nagas had probably shot her, for they liked monkey meat. He had found it clinging to the branch of a low tree.

"A tortoise, an owl, an anteater, an ape, and a python," sighed Phyllida happily. "Now we really have got a sanctuary."

"Where *is* the python?" said Annabelle.

The boy jerked his thumb toward the temple. The python was sunning itself on the tiles outside the door. It looked happy at last, but it was also a problem. Would it know it was in a sanctuary, and which things it could crush to death and which not?

"I told it," said the grandmother. "I rubbed the medicine in this morning. It will eat nothing until I tell it."

"It'll starve then," Phyllida complained.

"It will not starve," said the boy. "Pythons can go for months without eating."

They could not worry about this problem for long, for now there were two more mouths to feed and a tail to be doctored. The grandmother dealt with the anteater's tail using the leaves which had cured Phyllida's scratches. It did not take its head from its paws. In spite of its armor-plated body and the tigerish claws on its front feet, it seemed shy and helpless.

"It'll eat ants, that's easy," said Annabelle, but it seemed that it would only eat ants' eggs. However, the boy knew plenty of places where these could be found.

The ape was more difficult.

"It must have milk," said the boy. "We can give it a little from our cow but we do not have much."

"We can bring a bottle every day," said Phyllida. "I can ask the cowman to give it to me without telling Mummy." They also had the old feeding bottle Miranda had used, so that seemed to solve the problem of the feeding; but where were the new animals to be housed?

"The ape must stay with someone day and night," the boy insisted. "It needs the warmth of a body. These apes stay with their mothers till they are a year old."

"My body's warmest," Annabelle declared.

"Mummy would never let you," said Phyllida, "so forget it."

This, she sadly decided, was true. The little gray ape might be allowed to stay with them for part of the time, but during school and at night it would be banished.

"I will keep it," said the boy.

"That's all very well . . ." began Annabelle peevishly, but Phyllida interrupted:

"He's right, Bella. We can play with it in the daytime, but at night it must stay with him. We can't leave it here by itself."

For the anteater the only place seemed the temple again. A week under the eye of the image with plenty of ants' eggs and soothing leaves on its tail, and it would feel secure; the python would have to be locked out till the two got used to each other. They hoped that as it settled down it would smell less strongly. Candy was trembling so much at the powerful waves of anteater that were wafting across to her that she had to be picked up and soothed.

The August days were hardly long enough to collect Lengra's leaves, Walt's meat, ants' eggs, and milk. They brought water from the pond in hollow bamboo pipes and dug another small pond in the glade so that at least the python could drink, since it ate nothing. Then they had to think of names. After a lot of argument they called the python Pompey and the anteater Alexander because they had been reading about these people in school. The little ape they called Poo because one or the other of them was always tickling its round stomach and saying, "Well, monkey *poo?*"

Poo was everyone's favorite. At first he clung to the boy's side like a gray burr, digging his pointed fingers into the boy's shoulders and screaming shrilly if anyone tried to dislodge him. He learned to suck milk from the bottle without any difficulty, and the sight of it produced a deep belching noise, which rose to a scream if he did not get the milk quickly. He sucked with his toes curling, like a baby.

Gradually he grew more friendly, and would let Phyllida or Annabelle carry him. He was warm, but light as fluff. His head fitted into Phyllida's hand and his ears were like small black snails stuck to the sides of his skull. His pointed fingers pulled apart leaves and insects, gently tugged at everyone's eyelashes, and scratched the small of his back. When Candy came close enough he poked her, which made her scream and rush off; she was the only animal who positively disliked the sanctuary.

Alexander the anteater licked up the ants' eggs they put for him in the temple and his tail healed. His slanting eyes stayed shy and he spent a lot of the time curled up with his nose between his paws.

"Pangolins do," said Phyllida, who had looked him up in her animal book and found his proper name.

But when his tail had healed she said, "We must

let him out. This isn't supposed to be a zoo. It's a sanctuary."

"We keep Lengra in a cage," Annabelle pointed out.

"Yes, but it takes him most of the day to walk round it. Alexander needs more room, and he needs to use his claws. I found him trying to dig a hole in the floor yesterday."

The boy agreed, and the grandmother said it was quite simple, she would rub some of her medicine into him. They doubted whether any medicine, however magical, would get through the anteater's scales, but they allowed her to try. They had become fond of the grandmother, and missed her on the days when she was not jangling and shouting around the glade. They even ate with pleasure the sweetmeats she brought, and did not notice any signs of being spellbound.

So next morning, the medicine rubbed, the door was opened and Alexander strolled out. Pompey the python was up the peepul tree, Lengra was in his cage, Poo was fastened to the boy's hip, and Walt was on the grandmother's shoulder. Phyllida held the trembling Candy in her arms and Annabelle had decided to roll in the clearing like a horse.

They had laid some ant heaps invitingly around the glade, and these Alexander sniffed at as he waddled past, but he did not stop to eat. He looked like some monster out of the Ice Age, with his scaly body and his stumpy tail dragging behind him. He walked like a giant lizard too, lopsidedly with his shoulders rolling. He walked past Lengra's cage, and the peepul tree, and the group of silent figures, into the jungle. They watched his maimed tail slide out of sight and for a moment there was crackling, then silence.

"So," said Annabelle to the grandmother, "that's how good your medicine was!"

Phyllida sniffed and found the glade had become blurred.

"He may come back," she said in a watery voice.

"Of course he will come back," shouted the grandmother. "My medicine never fails. Never."

"He smelled terrible." Annabelle tried to find some way of making the best of what had happened.

"I liked his smell," Phyllida lied.

"You would," said Annabelle.

"Why would I?"

"Because you smell yourself, I suppose."

But Phyllida was too sad to carry on the argument, and in spite of a story from the grandmother about the war between men and monkeys, and her promise of a black panther to take Alexander's place, they left for breakfast with long faces.

It was not only that they missed the anteater, smell

and all. It was the knowledge that their sanctuary had failed to please him. For the first time the temple and its keepers had not charmed a creature who had entered the circle of their protection. Brindaban was just another jungle to the anteater.

When they came back in the afternoon neither the boy nor his grandmother was there. Only Lengra and Pompey shared the sleepy afternoon air.

"We'd better get rid of the ants' eggs," said Phyllida. "They mess the place up."

"Funny," said Annabelle, "something's eaten them."

The earth hills were scattered and broken, and not an egg was left.

"Birds, probably," said Phyllida.

They threw the dry earth away and swept with their bamboo brushes. Then they took their pots to the spring to get water to wash out the temple.

"Gosh, you must admit Alexander did stink," gasped Annabelle as they carried the water through the temple door. "We'll never get it. . . . Help! He's *here*."

"Who's here?" said Phyllida, who was following; but the next second she had let out a happy scream. Alexander was lying curled up with his nose in his paws, just under the image and the butter lamps.

"*Alexander*," cried Phyllida, dropping her pot and running over to the sleeping anteater. She wanted

to stroke him, but apart from his soft nose, which
was hidden, there was nothing strokable about him.
She noticed that his claws were muddy.

"He's had a good dig," she said dreamily. "That's
what you wanted, wasn't it? And now you've come
back to your home, you clever sweet old anteater."

"Honestly," said Annabelle, "if you knew how
soppy you sounded."

"Ai-ee." The boy had come up behind them, and
made them both jump. "He is back, old brother
anteater. My grandmother's medicine was not so
bad after all, was it?"

They left Alexander to sleep off his dig, and went
out into the sunshine. Annabelle galloped around
the glade neighing, while Phyllida and the boy
played with Poo on the peepul tree. He was beginning to swing on his sticks of arms, but if they
moved a foot away from him he screamed and hurled
himself at whoever was closest.

Phyllida felt a great swelling sense of happiness.
The real Brindaban could not have been better than
this, and none of this would have been possible without the boy. Watching him now with his white
teeth flashing and the sun glinting red in his hair, she
knew that this was how the real Krishna must have
looked as a boy. Like the real Krishna he had taken
into his care all the troubled creatures of the forest
around him.

The boy was almost like a god himself, with his knowledge and skill and tenderness, and he had made her dreams of the sanctuary come true. Pompey on his branch, Lengra in his shaded run, Alexander under the eye of the image, and Poo swinging and somersaulting within reach of her hand completed the lovely pattern of the temple and the peepul tree. Only Miranda was missing, and the blue god himself.

"I know when he will come," she said suddenly, speaking her thoughts.

"Who will come?"

"The blue god. On the full moon of the night that ends the summer. That was when he danced with the milkmaids beside the river Jumna. When is the full moon that ends the summer?"

The boy calculated: there would be this full moon, at the end of August, and the next one would be the moon that ended the summer.

"Quite close," said Phyllida. "We shall have to come here that night."

"We shall have many more animals by then," said the boy. "We shall have a black panther."

Phyllida thought this was unlikely. Black panthers were very rare, and to find one injured or deserted would be a miracle.

"My grandmother is making a spell now," said the boy. "Her spells never fail."

Phyllida wondered if it was fair to put a panther under a spell to become wounded, but the thought came and went. Spell or no spell, black panthers were so rare that even the grandmother could not produce one.

"Your grandmother is very clever but she will fail this time," Phyllida said.

But she was wrong.

twelve

The Terrible Truth

FOR THREE DAYS the grandmother stayed away making her spells, Walt with her. He could now fly, and the grandmother had taught him, just as the mother owl taught her children, how to pounce on small scuttling creatures for his food. They could imagine how like a mother owl the grandmother must look to Walt.

Alexander came and went. They left the temple door open at night, and when he was out they scrubbed it with soap; but his powerful smell could not be drowned by carbolic, or frangipani flowers, or the sticks of scented wood the boy brought for them to burn. Through the sweetness and sourness and woodiness the odor of pangolin persisted. They were so glad to have him back, though, that they did not mind and continued to collect ants' eggs for him to add to the ones he found on his own.

Pompey slept and slid and continued to starve.

He was thinner than when he arrived but showed no interest in food. The grandmother took her spell off him, and the boy brought a chicken which perched on the python as if he were a log. He never hissed or showed his teeth, and they felt no fear of him, nor he of them. Poo belched with surprise when first they introduced the two, but was soon leaning over to poke the snake's dry decorated body. Lengra paced his cage, planning new tricks to play on the tiger.

On the fourth morning the grandmother, Walt, the boy, and a basket were waiting for them. In all their eyes was excitement and expectancy.

"Another small thing!" cried Phyllida. "Dibs I open it."

"Take care," said the boy as she wrenched at the bamboo that bound the lid. "It is small but it can bite."

A loud hissing was coming from the basket. Phyllida paused.

"It's not a snake?" she asked.

"Open it, open it," shouted the grandmother.

"Let me see," complained Annabelle.

"Take care," said the boy. "Just a crack."

Phyllida drew open the lid an inch or two and waited. There was silence from the basket. Very carefully she eased the lid farther off, and she and Annabelle bumped heads as they leaned forward to peer in. Both of them drew in their breaths in a long sigh of wonder and astonishment.

At the bottom of the basket, curled up, but raising closed eyes and a spitting mouth—tiny, perfect, impossible—was a black panther. The dark silky skin showed the rosettes of its leopard coat, but that it was as black as a panther could be, there was no doubt.

It was a kitten, not more than a few days old. Its ears were flat to its head and it spat like a firework. Its feet were large for the rest of its body, and the pointed claws were out.

"A black panther," breathed Phyllida. "Just like the *Jungle Book*. Bagheera for Brindaban."

"Super," said Annabelle.

"I told you," said the boy.

"My medicine," crowed the grandmother. "I can get you anything you wish for. You would like a rhinoceros! I can get it."

But they wanted nothing more for the moment. Later perhaps a golden tiger to slink beside their leopard; but for now their wildest dream was coiled up, hostile and frightened and probably hungry, in the basket at their feet. They closed the lid and sat in a wondering silence. Even the grandmother was quiet for once, though her yellow eyes shone with pleasure and pride.

It was Annabelle who jerked them back from their

*153

daydreams by saying, "I hope it doesn't scream so that its mother hears it and comes roaring along to get it."

"Oh, its mother will never hear it," said the boy confidently. "Its lair is a long way away. I was very careful. . . ."

He paused, and there was a silence in which Phyllida could hear her blood come roaring up and drum against her ears. Then it drained away and she thought she was going to be sick. The glade turned a peculiar shade of green, and her throat went tight. At last she found her voice, though only a faint one.

"You stole it from its lair?" she said.

The boy looked defiant.

"There were three more," he said. "This was the only black one. His mother will never miss him. She has a black cub every year."

Now Phyllida knew why the boy and his grandmother were able to say with such certainty, "I will get you a black panther." They knew where the mother leopard lived, where anteaters lived, owls nested, and how to catch a tortoise by one of its slow fat legs. As for Poo, she knew and they knew that the only way to get a baby ape away from its mother's body was to have the mother dead, and then pull. . . .

For the first time since she had found the temple,

the magic drained out of the glade, and she saw it as it really was: a ruin, some grass, and some animals which, through the boy's treachery, were forced into it to live maimed and stunted lives. She turned on him with her eyes blazing.

"How could you?" she said in a voice between a sob and a shriek. "You knew this was a sanctuary. You trapped them all, didn't you? Pompey too. How did you manage to hurt him enough to get him here?"

"It had just eaten," said the boy, his chin out. "It was sleepy. You wanted animals for your sanctuary so I brought them."

"We'll have to let them all go," said Phyllida, half sobbing. "This isn't a sanctuary any more. It's a prison."

"They won't go," said Annabelle sensibly. "They like it here."

It was true. Neither Pompey nor Alexander seemed to want to leave, nor Walt. Poo was too small to fend for himself; there was only Lengra. Very dramatically Phyllida went and threw open the door of his cage, but he was dozing and did not notice.

"What is the matter, my darlings?" said the grandmother who had not been able to follow their talk. "Don't you like the panther? Is it too small? I will get you an elephant. . . ."

The boy turned to her, and in a language they did not understand spoke rapidly for a couple of minutes. When the grandmother looked at them again her eyes were like chips of yellow glass. She turned and left the glade, but they did not notice her go.

A faint mewing from the basket made them remember the cause of all the trouble.

"The kitten must go back anyway," Phyllida announced. "Now, before his mother misses him."

"I will take him back," said the boy, snatching up the basket.

"I will come with you," said Phyllida.

The boy knew that she did not trust him to return the kitten, and she did not care that he knew. He picked up the basket, jerked his head, and said, "Come." With flaming cheeks Phyllida followed him down the path which led to the spring, and on into deeper jungle which she had never explored before. Candy bobbed in front and Annabelle plodded behind.

It was a hot morning and sweat stood out on their foreheads as they pushed their way through the stinging grass. Spiders' webs stuck to their faces and bamboo stems whipped against their legs; but Phyllida did not notice any of these things. She was in such a rage of disappointment and grief over the spoiled sanctuary that she felt nothing except a pain in her throat and a black hate against the boy that

156*

seemed to darken the very air. It was not until he stopped suddenly and put a finger to his lips that a new feeling woke in her—fear.

Then it struck her that this was a very foolish thing they were doing. It was in fact a terribly dangerous thing. A mother leopard whose cub they carried might be waiting for them anywhere in this thick jungle. One loud mew from the kitten and a snarling form would hurl itself out of the dense thatch grass, and raking claws would punish them for the unpardonable sin of the wild—to take a helpless cub from its lair. The sweat on her forehead turned to icy drops, and she picked up Candy.

They were in a pathless jumble of trees, bamboos, and coiling creepers which snaked and hung from every trunk and stem. Each step was a pushing, a snapping, a bending under or crawling over. No sunlight penetrated the green curtain of leaf and stalk, and there was a strong rank smell, a mixture of mushrooms and old grass mowings. The boy had dropped to his knees and was inching forward almost soundlessly, putting the basket down and then picking it up again, easing his legs into the sodden ground.

Phyllida turned around and saw Annabelle's ashen face behind her. Candy gave a little moan, and she closed her hand over her muzzle. The boy stopped to turn and frown, then waited for them to creep up and join him. The crackle of their feet seemed deafening.

"We are almost at the place," he whispered when they joined him. "There is a thick clump of thatch just beyond that tree, and in it is a hollow log. In the log is the lair. You must wait here and I will put the cub back. If you hear a noise, run."

Phyllida shook her head. The boy was not going to risk his life while she ran. Besides, if they lost him they would themselves be lost.

"We will come too," she breathed. "If you go we go."

Annabelle nodded, her eyes enormous.

"It is too dangerous," said the boy. "The mother is near. I can run faster than you. I can climb a tree."

"So can a leopard," said Phyllida.

"I have my knife," said the boy, fingering the square bladed axe he carried.

But Phyllida shook her head firmly. It seemed as if she must do this terrible, terrifying thing to make up for Poo's dead mother and Lengra's leg, and the anteater's tail.

"Very well," whispered the boy, "but do not make the smallest sound. The mother is near," and he lifted his nose and smelled the air. Then, inch by inch, he began to creep forward.

Phyllida could not crawl because of Candy, who

was now in a frenzy of shaking. She lifted each heel and put it down as if she were walking on eggs, and felt each tiny snap of twig as if it were a pistol shot. Sometimes she had to bend double, and once she got her hair caught in a branch, and with shaking fingers Annabelle unwrapped each strand.

When after what seemed like an hour they reached the tree the boy had pointed out, he squatted on his haunches, beckoning them to do the same. There was a small clear space and opposite it the thatch where the hollow log and the leopard's lair were. They crouched with their backs to the tree and stared at the thatch. It flickered in front of their eyes like green snakes.

Then very slowly the boy started to unwind the bamboo from the lid of the basket. They took their eyes from the thatch to watch him, and then switched them back hastily in case they missed a parting in the stems and a leopard face peering out. Once or twice they glanced up into the tree in case a spotted body lay along a branch. A leopard was the wiliest of the wild creatures; it would come up from behind or fall from above. It would do the thing least expected of it.

At last the lid of the basket was loosened and gently eased free. Then came the most difficult part, the lifting of the kitten. They knew how it would feel, clasped in naked man hands, the same

*159

hands that had wrenched it from its mother's body and thrust it into an emptiness where there was neither warmth nor food. They knew it would struggle.

The boy's hand hovered in the mouth of the basket, and grabbed. There was a hissing, a scrabbling, and he had the kitten out and hanging by the scruff of its neck, claws waving wildly. There was blood on his arm. His other hand whipped around to close the cub's mouth, but he was a fraction of a second too late. It gave a loud, terrified wail.

Then everything happened at once. The thatch opposite opened, there was a snarl, a spotted body, the kitten flying through the air. Candy yelped, the boy shouted "run" and as if the jungle were an open road they turned and sped through it. Their hearts were beating so loudly they could not hear if the leopard were just behind them. They ran until there was no more breath in their bodies, and they had to fall on their faces in the grass and wait to be sprung upon.

Their ears roared, their chests ached, and for several minutes they could hear nothing, feel nothing except their own panic and exhaustion. Then gradually the noises of the jungle returned through their wheezing breath: birds, the high-pitched hum of crickets, and the boy's voice saying, "It will not come now. We must go back."

They struggled to their feet to follow him, dazed and trembling as much as Candy. Their legs felt like flannel, and they stumbled, scratching themselves and moaning, not from pain but to rid themselves of their fear. With every step they felt happier, and by the time they reached the glade their hearts were beating normally again, and a warmth was beginning to spread over them at the thought of how brave they had been. Even Candy looked quite jaunty.

They went to the spring first, to drink and drink, and lay their foreheads and cheeks in the cold water. When they had lain for several minutes examining each other's scratches and moaning again, but this time with pleasure, Annabelle said, "We'll be terribly late. Gosh, we'll be *hours* late."

To their surprise their adventure had only taken an hour. They would be late, but it could be explained away. They wondered, though, what their mother would say if they casually mentioned that they had just confronted a leopard in its lair. They felt braver every minute.

They rose a little stiffly and went back to the glade to say goodbye to the boy, but he had gone. Pompey was piled up on the warm tiles in front of the temple. Lengra had not yet discovered he was free and was nibbling contentedly in his cage. Alexander was out. They suddenly thought of Poo; the grandmother must have taken him. The morning had been so full, so confused, hurtful and thrilling, that they could not sort out all that had happened.

They both slept all afternoon and awakened to talk drowsily of that incredible moment when the leopard had sprung from the thatch and the cub, hurled by the boy, had been snatched up in her jaws with a cry between a growl and a purr. It was nice to think of the family together again: the baby black panther safe in the circle of thatch and the curving gold body of his mother.

"I wasn't all that frightened," said Phyllida, "I could do it again easily."

"Me too," said Annabelle. "Easily."

"I'm glad we didn't keep the little leopard. We couldn't have taught it how to kill before we went to school in England."

"We couldn't have taught it how to kill ever," said Annabelle. "Could we?"

"The grandmother probably could have," said Phyllida. She thought about this, and smiled, imagining the lessons and the grandmother shouting, "Not like that my darling, EAT it," to the black panther.

She did not mind thinking of the grandmother, but when she thought of the boy the back of her throat ached. She would never forget the sick moment when she understood that he had not charmed the animals into her life, simply dragged them. He had made the sanctuary, and spoiled the sanctuary.

Yet had he spoiled it? Nothing could spoil the peace of the peepul tree spilling its shadows on the temple roof. Nothing could spoil the patterns on Pompey's skin, or Poo's ears, like curled black ferns, or the anteater's shy and slanting eyes. She would never have known about these things without the boy.

"Perhaps the riddle will explain it all," thought Phyllida.

But the lump stayed in the back of her throat, and was still there when she went back to the sanctuary in the morning. The boy was not there—not that day, nor the day after, nor the day after that. A week went by and still the boy did not come back.

thirteen

The Right White Stone

AT FIRST Phyllida and Annabelle pretended they were quite happy to have the glade to themselves. They asked the malis for ants' eggs, and they found that Alexander liked milk so they gave him what they brought for Poo. Lengra dozed and munched and made no more effort to leave the glade than Pompey. There were always jobs to be done, for the grass grew inches in the warmth and wetness, the spring had to be built up, the temple floor to be washed and polished, and fresh flowers picked for the image.

Nevertheless as August ended and the September days passed and still there was no boy, no Poo, no grandmother or Walt, they began to grow anxious.

"If only we knew where they lived," said Phyllida. They had never thought of asking this; the two had just appeared from the jungle and gone back through it to a house with a cow and a patch of rice.

*165

"It's your fault for being so cross with him," said Annabelle. "The grandmother's probably brewing up spells against us with Walt's blood this very minute."

"Don't be silly," said Phyllida, but a little uneasily. Thinking it over, she regretted her anger on that day of the black panther. The boy had meant well, he had wanted to please her, no more. He had taken the little leopard from its lair as a gesture of love; he had risked his life to bring her what he thought she most wanted. And in return she had betrayed him.

She missed him more than she would have thought possible. She missed the skill of his hands in shaping wood, his bright noticing eyes, and his lips that could shape themselves to call birds and cicadas and could tell her why they called. As the quarter moon appeared she felt panic-stricken. This was the moon that ended the summer. He must be back in Brindaban when it was full.

Another week passed. The rice was a deep green and filled the patch. Ayah wrote to say her auntie was no longer lying like a log and that she would be back at the end of the month. Both these things pleased them, but the boy's absence was like a faintly aching tooth, spoiling everything they did.

Annabelle decided she had been neglecting her ponies and did not go to the glade in the morning. Sometimes she slept through the afternoon as well.

She had the rubber bit back in her mouth and was no longer a wild stallion. She was a show jumper and trotted around and around with red ribbons tied to her forehead.

"The boy will never come back," she said, and shied violently, knocking over all the jumps at the International Horse Show.

Phyllida continued to go to the glade to see Alexander and Lengra and Pompey, and to hope that the boy would be there. One early morning in mid-September she left Annabelle mucking out the stables and set off with her ants' eggs and the bottle of milk for the anteater. Poo would probably be eating bananas by now, and wild figs. She wondered if he were darkening, and whether he could walk. She missed his pouting welcomes, his dry gentle fingers and soft clean fur, but she knew he would be happy with the boy.

When she got to the glade there was the moment of hope, the search for footprints, and the disappointment. She went first, as she always did, to see the image and to find out if Alexander were at home. She remembered the day she had found the temple and how beautiful it had seemed, mysterious and secret. She had wanted to keep it for herself, but she had been wrong. It had grown more beautiful with the boy and the animals in it; even the grandmother had added her funny noisy charm.

Alexander was out but there was mud on the floor to show he had been there. Phyllida swept it absently, poured his milk into the bowl she had kept for him, and carried the ants' eggs outside to lay on the step. Lengra was back in his cage and Pompey curled up just outside it. Phyllida bent to scratch his back but he did not stir. His skin looked loose on him now, but there was nothing they could do to make him eat.

She went to the spring next, to look for signs of Miranda. There had been no deer prints for some time, and there were none this morning. She sat for a few minutes picking leaves and grass from the water, and also a struggling moth. It was green and silver with a pattern of black lines and dots around the edges of its wings. The boy would have known a story to explain the pattern. She jumped quickly to her feet and shook off the thought of the boy.

She had only Lengra to provide for now, and wandered down the path that led to the patch of leaves he liked. The first time she had used it was when the boy had shown them the spring; the last time when they had returned the black panther. It was no good, she decided, trying to shut the boy out of her mind, because every inch of the jungle carried memories of him.

It was this path the three of them had crept down to catch the bhoot that was really his grandmother.

It was around this corner they had peered, and under that tree that she had seen the bent old woman grinding what she had thought were bones, there on that big white stone.

"White stone," said Phyllida aloud, and paused, and frowned. Of course! *This* was the white stone that had lain at the bottom of her mind whenever she thought of the riddle. How silly of her not to remember it; it was so large, a boulder more than a stone, and so much whiter than any other rocks in the jungle. She bent over it, trying to find some message or sign on its surface.

There seemed to be nothing. The stone was smooth, egg-shaped, and ordinary, except in its whiteness. She ran her fingers over it. There were no bumps or patterns, no sword to be plucked out, no crack to split open and show gold. It might be a beautiful maiden bewitched, but if so she did not know the words to free her.

She sat down on the stone and laid her palms flat on its cold surface repeating the riddle slowly:

"What is deeper than root of the tal-sal tree?
 What is darker than porcupine's burrow?
 Seek a white stone, seek a white stone,
 Will spiders' eggs bring you sorrow?"

Her eyes were fixed on the ground in front of the

stone, but her thoughts were on the words; so that it was not for several minutes that she noticed something strange about the earth she was staring at. The strangeness was not strange though, it was familiar.

Clearly marked out on a specially smoothed patch of ground was a rectangle with some sticks arranged in it, like this.

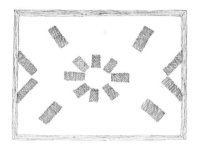

It was the other half of the riddle, the diagram the grandmother had drawn when she had told it to them. Now there was no doubt at all that somewhere within a few feet of where she was sitting was the answer to the secret of the temple and the glade.

She got up and walked slowly around the stone, prodding at the ground. She picked up the sticks, and ran her nail around the outside edge of the diagram, and put the sticks back and stared at them from every angle. Then she went back to the stone again and examined it inch by inch, working slowly toward the ground. She could see no connection between the diagram and the stone, or the stone and the riddle. She tapped the trunk of the tree behind it, but no door opened to reveal demon's treasure.

Then as she glanced at the stone again, she noticed something she had missed before. At one side, the side opposite the diagram, there were scraping marks on the ground. At once she knew what had made them. The stone had been moved. The treasure lay under it, or if not the treasure, another clue to it. Someone had recently pushed it aside. She must do the same.

This was a great deal more difficult, she soon realized, than it looked. The boulder was not only heavy, it was so smooth that it was hard to grasp anywhere, to get a hold that would help her to push or pull. She sat down, bent her knees, dug in her heels, and pushed with her back. She lay flat on her stomach with her feet against the tree trunk and heaved. She took a run and fell on it with a great grunting shove, but this only hurt her hands.

It seemed the only way to move it was to tell Annabelle and get her help, but this she did not want to do. Annabelle had scoffed at the secret and made silly suggestions about searching for porcupines' burrows. Phyllida wanted to discover the secret, and then hold her discovery over Annabelle's head and

*171

gloat. She looked around to see if there were any weapon she could use—a strong piece of wood perhaps, to lever the boulder up with.

Strangely, there was exactly what she had in mind propped against the trunk of the tree, though she had not previously noticed it. It was an old bit of iron; it looked like the rusted blade of one of the boy's square knives. He had probably put it there some time ago, and forgotten it. She grabbed it gleefully and immediately set to work to edge the white stone aside.

To her joy it moved. Very slowly she pressed on the iron lever, afraid it would break with the weight. She shifted one side of the stone a few inches, then the other. Then she edged the iron under the center of the boulder. For a second or two she strained without seeming to make an impression. Then slowly the stone lifted, hung, and half toppled over.

Phyllida staggered back with the weight suddenly gone from under her arms, then leaped forward. She had been right. Under the stone was a deep dark hole, the entrance to a cave or passage. She found her knees trembling with excitement. Treasure, of course! Gold galore, jewels and coins and silks! Annabelle would be simply furious.

She knelt down and peered into the hole. It was very dark and she could not see the bottom, but by leaning over and feeling with the piece of iron she found she could touch it. Gingerly she lowered her legs over the edge and slid down into the hole. Her head was below the surface of the ground and her feet rested on firm earth. There was no bag of gold beneath her sandals, but there was a passage. The light from above showed it to her as it sloped gently downward. Her fingers felt its opening. It was big enough to walk down, stooping slightly.

She started very slowly moving along it. When she had taken a few steps she realized it was soon going to be pitch dark, and felt for her box of matches. She always carried these to light the butter lamps in the temple. She lit one now and keeping it carefully steady edged her way on. But the match went out, and when she lit another it did the same. Better to have a butter lamp.

She was out of the hole, back along the path, into the temple and out again faster than she had ever run—except perhaps when flying from the leopard. Even so she kept the earthenware saucer steady so as not to spill the oil in it. She wished it carried more oil, but it would burn long enough to light her to the end of the passage.

The butter lamp flickered, but it stayed lit, and it was a comfort to have its glow. Phyllida was surprised to see that the passage was not made simply of earth, it was roofed and walled in the same tiles as the temple. The tiles were furred with dirt and moss, but their hardness pressed comfortingly against her feet. Slimy mud might have been a bit eerie.

The passage did not slope steeply, but it led clearly downhill. She was not sure how long she crept along it, stooping over, trying to shade the flame of the butter lamp from a draft that was trying to put it out. She only knew that suddenly there were no walls against her elbows or roof above her head. The lamp flame grew stronger as she lifted it and looked around.

She was in some sort of a room or cave. Her lamp showed her curving walls, tiled like the passage, and a roof which disappeared into a point, as did the temple's. In the center of the dim space there was a square raised shape, and from this a coil of faint smoke was rising. It smelled sweet and woody. It reminded her of the grandmother.

For the first time a tiny flutter of fear stirred in her stomach. She remembered the grandmother's eyes as she had last seen them, flakes of yellow glass, cold and sharp. Now here she was, alone with the secret that the two of them knew, alone in a hole under the ground with that odd little fire the grandmother must have lighted sending out its bittersweet smoke to welcome her. Or was it a welcome? Was it not more likely to be a spell?

I must go, thought Phyllida, but how can I go without discovering something? To have solved the riddle, and moved the stone, and found—what had she found? Nothing but a sort of underground temple, in which the grandmother probably worshipped one of her special devils. In spite of the drifting wood smoke, the place had the bat smell, the mushroom smell of deep jungle where sunlight never reached. This was natural, she knew; any underground cave would smell like this.

Yet this was not a cave, it was a building. The grandmother had not dug it, or lined it with bricks, or built that oblong boxlike erection in the middle on top of which the little fire of burning ashes smoldered. She moved forward to examine the brick box, keeping away from the woodsmoke as much as possible in case it was meant to bewitch her.

The lump was perfectly plain, solid, and uncarved. The answer to the riddle was probably inside it, Phyllida thought. But how did the grandmother know this? Obviously it had not been opened, unless there was a loose brick somewhere, or secret spring. What a strange place to keep secrets? Who on earth would build a sort of underground temple and inside a great sealed brick box? It must be very old, as old as the temple, since it was made with the same tiles. Who would think of sealing up a secret and leaving it to molder under the ground for hundreds of years?

Of course! Who else but the old kings of Assam

who were buried all over Bird God Hill in their mounds? This was a tomb, a tomb that nobody had discovered except the grandmother, and now herself. Inside the brick box there would be gold, glittering heaps of coins, and golden caskets, bedsteads, lamps, and swords. Ayah had often told her about the kings, and so had her mother. They were buried with all their most valuable things around them, but most of the graves had been found and dug up and the treasure stolen. This was probably the only one that had not.

She gave a deep sigh of relief and satisfaction. It was all clear now. The temple on top guarded the tomb, which guarded the treasure. With all that the tomb contained she could buy bullocks for herself, for the cook and his wife, for everyone. She could buy Ayah a big house in the hills; she could get Annabelle a show jumper and her mother and father a boat with cabins. For the boy and his grandmother she could buy rice land that rolled as far as the eye could see.

She sneezed from the smoke of the ashes and her eyes watered. This brought her to earth, and made her remember that she had been out for at least the hour and a half she was allowed before breakfast. There was nothing more she could do for the moment; she would have to get help in opening the tomb. She would be famous, she would be rich, she would buy a whole great zoo for Alexander and Pompey and Poo.

She started back up the passage, the lamp burning low. It was nearly out of oil but she would not need it much longer. She moved as fast as she could, humming under her breath. "A zoo for Poo," she chanted, and it sounded very loud and odd. "A zoo for Poo and Pompey too," she sang, and said to herself, "Gosh, that's a poem," and tried to fit Alexander into the next line. She was so absorbed that she bumped into the end of the passage before she realized she had reached it.

This couldn't be the end, though; there was no light from the entrance where she had rolled the stone away. Raising the butter lamp she looked up and saw that now there was no entrance. The stone had rolled back and was blocking her way out, blocking the light and sealing her in.

fourteen

Trapped

AT FIRST Phyllida simply felt annoyed. How foolish of her to leave the stone wobbling on the edge of the entrance hole, so that it fell back and would need to be moved all over again. She would be later than ever now. Equally foolishly she had left the iron bar outside so that now she had nothing to help push. Still, it should be easier to shift from underneath.

She put down the butter lamp carefully, and raised her arms to the stone. She could only just reach it and give a faint pressure. She stood on tiptoe and heaved with all her strength, but there was little weight behind her flattened palms, and the stone would not budge. She dropped her arms to her sides, panting, and at the same moment the butter lamp went out.

Phyllida stood in the dark with tears pricking her eyelids and thought about her situation. She was shut under the ground in a place that only one other

178*

person knew of, and that person was her enemy. She could shout all day and nobody would hear. Annabelle would bring a rescue party to the glade, but would they come here, and would they move the stone? Candy might lead them. Candy might sniff and scratch at the stone and give them the clue to her whereabouts. She might.

Phyllida swallowed the lump in her throat, bent to pick up the butter lamp, and headed slowly back down the passage. There she could breathe, and perhaps find something on which she could stand to help her move the stone. She still had the matches in her pocket and with care she could make them last through her search. Anything was better than just standing still in the dark.

The tomb was full of the smell of the burning wood and spices, and strangely it was a comforting smell. It reminded her that just above her head was the temple and the image and the flower windows letting in the sunshine onto the red tiled floor, perhaps onto Alexander as he slept a contented ant-filled sleep.

Pompey would be outside in the sun; he liked the morning warmth on his dry skin, but rolled into the shade of the peepul tree when it grew hot. Thinking of them, and of their quiet routine, made her feel calmer. Only Lengra, waiting for his leaves, might be a little fretful.

She lit a match and, carefully shielding the flame, started slowly around the walls. They were furred like the passage with moss, and thinking of spiders she kept her fingers off them. She moved the match up and down, trying to find something movable, some loose bricks or a piece of broken stone which she could carry back to stand on. She used five matches before she found herself back at the passage again, and as the fifth match went out, her spirits sank with it.

With trembling fingers she counted the matches left in the box. There were four. She would use two of them to examine the brick altar in the center of the tomb, two she would keep. To be without even a match in the middle of the earth would be more than she could bear. Resolutely she moved forward, and when her fingers met the brick of the lump that rose from the floor of the tomb, she lit one of her matches.

She looked first at the little pile of ash on top, which had stopped smoking. There might be a small piece of wood she could light. But it seemed that the grandmother only used bones and blood and the milk of black and white cows for her fires, for there was nothing. "You haven't put *me* under your spell," she said out loud to the ashes, and her voice boomed back at her from the pointed roof. Her hand shook as she slowly moved it across the top of the bricks under which lay the treasure she had discovered at such cost.

The second match took her around the outside of the altar. She prodded and kicked, trying to pry loose a brick or find a secret opening. She went down onto her knees and felt along the frill of bricks that stuck out from the bottom. She was down on her knees when her match went out.

She stayed down, the stone floor cutting into her knees. She desperately wanted to light another match; her fingers clutched at the box, pushed it open, then closed it again. She must keep two matches. She must. She leaned forward and laid her forehead on the edge of the brick, and let tears of fear and failure flow down her cheeks and drop to the floor of the tomb.

It was no use, no use. The grandmother had closed the door of the passage, had lighted the bewitching fire, had imprisoned her forever for being so angry over the little black leopard. The boy did not know the answer to the riddle. She was more lost than she had been in the jungle at midnight, beyond the call of anyone, even of the blue god.

She lifted her head from the brick and sniffed. Just above her was Brindaban, whose magic was more powerful than the grandmother's. No human ears would hear her if she called, but could the Lord Krishna be listening? He had listened that full moon night when she had gone in search of Miranda. It would be worth calling him, just in case. Very softly, so as not to start the booming echo, she spoke his name.

"Lord Krishna," she whispered, "I am very sorry but I am lost again. Please will you push the stone away. I will never trouble you again if you will help me this time. Please push the stone."

She waited on her knees for a moment, then rose stiffly and prepared to light a match to find her way back to the passage. But before her fingers had slid open the tray in which her last two matches lay, there fell on her astonished ears the sound she knew to be the most beautiful in the world—a sound impossible in this place, a sound gentle, gay and soothing, a sound that turned the tomb, as it had turned the midnight jungle, into a haven of peace—the sound of a flute.

Warmth flowed over her and the dark walls were like arms around her. But where was the music coming from? It must be the passage, Krishna must have opened the entrance and be piping to her from the white stone. She lit a match with fingers that trembled now with joy, and it showed her the entrance to the passage; but strangely the faint fluting came from the opposite side of the tomb. She hesitated. Should she go back up the passage, or should she try to follow the music?

In fact she seemed to have little choice. The flute drew her toward it, leading her to what seemed to be a blank wall. She put out her fingers gingerly to touch a patch of moss, and found they slipped through. Naturally, why had she not thought of it—another entrance. Eagerly she wrenched at the curtain of moss and cobwebs that hung in front of it. As she did so, faint light reached her, revealing instead of a passage a steep flight of stairs. The match burned her fingers, and she dropped it and pulled with both hands to free the doorway that led to freedom and the flute player.

Then she was climbing on all fours, her hands and feet slipping on the wet surface of the steps. They were very narrow, but as it grew lighter and the flute continued to play, her heart nearly burst with excitement. This time there was no doubt at all that she would meet the blue god.

The top of the staircase was partly covered with the roots of a tree, and she had to force her way through them. Rising at last to her feet, she saw it was the peepul tree whose roots she had climbed through; and on another root, his legs crossed, his head thrown back, his flute to his smiling lips, sat the boy. Phyllida burst into tears, but whether of relief or disappointment she did not know.

The boy dropped his flute and jumped to his feet. "Eesh, where did you come from?" he cried.

Phyllida pointed to the hole she had crawled through and the boy went over to examine it. She was crouching with her head between her knees, sobbing so bitterly that she could not speak. The boy whistled between his teeth as he peered down the hole at the staircase. Then he came back to where Phyllida was sitting, and pushed her shoulder.

"Why do you cry?" he asked. "Why do you howl like a jackal?"

"I thought"—Phyllida lifted a soggy face—"I thought you were Krishna."

"Well, who else am I?" said the boy.

"The blue god, I mean."

"Ah, I see." The boy picked up his flute. "Because of this?"

Phyllida nodded, hiccuped, and then for no reason began to howl again. A hairy body suddenly dropped on her, and spider arms were around her neck. It was Poo, squeaking and smiling his frightened smile, laying his square teeth to her arm to show his panic at her tears.

"See," said the boy. "Even the snake will be scared if you continue to make such a noise."

He took Poo from Phyllida and rubbed a hand up and down the tiny monkey spine to soothe him.

"Why do you cry?" he repeated. "Since **you** have solved the riddle?"

*185

"You know about the riddle?" Phyllida lifted a startled face again.

"My grandmother told me on the day of the black panther. We wanted to do something to make you happy, since we had made you sad. So we helped you to solve the riddle. Every day we made the signs on the ground by the white stone, and put the knife near by, but you never saw them. Until today."

"Until today," Phyllida repeated. She was dazed. The tomb and its gold had been a peace offering. The fire had been a welcoming one, a friendly sign, an assurance that someone had been there before, but there was the stone.

"The stone," said Phyllida out loud. "Someone pushed it back. I couldn't get out."

"It must have fallen," said the boy. "My grandmother would never have pushed it. We would have seen that it had been moved, and come to free you. There was no danger."

He spoke as if being trapped underground in a pitch dark tomb were an everyday occurrence.

"And what did you think of the secret?" he asked.

Phyllida wiped her hand across her cheeks, and thought about the gold that lay under her feet, and thought about Annabelle's face when she saw it. She was so busy imagining how pink and jealous this would be that she did not hear the sound of approaching footsteps; and when the real face was suddenly in front of her she jumped.

"Gosh," spluttered Annabelle. "Where have you *been?* Daddy's got the whole labor force out looking for you."

Phyllida leaped up.

"Wow!" she exclaimed, "I forgot about the time. What did you tell them? You didn't say anything about this place, did you?"

Annabelle flung herself on the grass panting.

"I had an *awful* time," she complained. "I told terrible lies. I had to. If I go to hell it'll be all your fault. They've gone into the hills and they're expecting to find you've been kidnapped and Mummy says she won't let us go out on our own ever again." She sat up. "And where have *you* been?" she demanded of the boy peevishly. "You might have let us know instead of just disappearing With Poo and Walt as well."

"I'll tell you everything when we get home," Phyllida said. "Come on, let's hurry."

"*Hurry,*" Annabelle squeaked, "I've been hurrying for the last two hours while you've just been. . . ." She paused and looked puzzled.

"What *have* you been doing? I came here before and you weren't here then."

"I'll tell you when we get home." Phyllida

grabbed her arm. "It's the most exciting thing you ever imagined. It's the secret of Brindaban."

Annabelle got up and looked from Phyllida to the boy, pawing the ground suspiciously.

"You've solved the riddle?" she asked.

"Yes."

"The boy told you?"

"No, by myself."

Annabelle's face was as pink with envy as Phyllida had imagined. She stood eyeing them and breathing deeply. Then she tossed her head and whinnied derisively.

"H'm, h'm, h'm, who cares?" she snorted, galloping off down the path toward home. "Silly old secret. Just wait till Daddy gets hold of you."

Phyllida made a face at the boy and he shrugged.

"It'll be all right," she said. "I'll be back."

"Of course. On Sunday it is the night of the full moon."

"I'll be back in the morning," Phyllida said, turning to call to him. "We'll talk about it then. Please thank your grandmother."

The boy answered with a trill on his flute, and the sound comforted her as she ran through the hot morning air to the terrible row that she knew awaited her.

They were indeed very angry, angrier than she

had ever seen them. They said the things she expected about frightening everyone to death and wasting hundreds of dollars by using the laborers on the tea garden to search for her; and they said the one thing she dreaded, that she would not be allowed to go out on her own in the future. She was sent to bed for the morning and lay in the darkened room under the fan, like a prisoner under a life sentence.

At break time Annabelle came in with some lime juice. They sipped it gloomily, and Phyllida told of the solving of the riddle and the discovery of the treasure.

"But what about the porcupines and the spiders' eggs?" Annabelle asked.

"Well, the tomb was dark like a porcupine's burrow, wasn't it?" said Phyllida. "And spiders' eggs, well, they're gold, aren't they? It's easy really." In fact she had only just thought of these solutions herself and Annabelle knew it.

"It was just a fluke your finding it," she said. "And anyway, what's the use of a treasure when we can't get at it? It serves you right really, for leaving me out."

"I'll get the treasure out somehow," Phyllida told her. "And I won't let you have any of it."

"I'd like to see you try," said Annabelle, cantering off to school and leaving Phyllida bouncing furiously up and down on her sticky bed.

Lunch was a miserable meal and included spinach soup, an extra punishment they felt sure. Afterward they went back to their bedroom again and fell into deep despairing sleeps. They were awakened by yaps and shrieks, the yaps from Candy, the shrieks from Ayah.

She ran to their beds, to hug their hot sleepy shoulders and kiss their creased cheeks.

"Darlings, my darlings," she cooed. "I coming back. I sending letter. Getting?"

"Not," said Phyllida, blinking. She was very glad to see Ayah but too hot and dazed to show it. She allowed herself to be hugged and examined for stings and snakebites, and Annabelle said, "You bringing lots honey," in a gruff voice to hide her shyness.

"Lots honey," said Ayah. "Lots porks. Come, getting dressed, washed, habing tea, I telling eberyting."

So while they ate the honey from her auntie's bees Ayah described the other auntie's illness, and they told her how often they had washed their hair and of the snakes they had just missed treading on. It was not until they were in bed again that night that they were able to consider Brindaban, the treasure, and the boy.

"You know," said Phyllida, "we'll have to tell Ayah. We can't go out without her. We'll have to take her there."

"We promised," Annabelle reminded her. "We swore on the boy's tiger tooth we wouldn't tell anyone else."

"He'll understand. It's either that or not going at all. She might even like it, you never know."

"She'll be simply scared to death," Annabelle declared. "She'll tell Mummy about the python. And the image, she'll have fits about the image. She'll scream and say, 'White peoples not doing like dat.'"

Phyllida knew this was true, and thought for a moment.

"We'll tell her we're going to England and she'll never see us again ever, and make her so miserable she'll promise to help us," she announced at last.

And thinking over this scheme they fell asleep happier than they had been all day.

fifteen

The Full Moon that Ended the Summer

A<small>YAH</small> did scream when they took her to the glade next day, but it was a scream of surprise more than horror. A smiling image and a sleeping python side by side in the middle of thick jungle was so unexpected that she dropped her knitting. When the boy and his grandmother arrived with Poo and Walt there were more screams, and a lot of explanations; and then suddenly Ayah and the grandmother were sitting side by side chattering and laughing and examining the contents of their waist bags.

They were both hill women and were soon chewing the grandmother's jelly and giggling about the stupidity of the people who lived on the plains. Phyllida, Annabelle, and the boy took Poo to the peepul tree and talked in whispers about the treasure.

"We'll have to tell Ayah if we're going to dig it

192*

up," Annabelle said. "Let's tell her now and then we can go and look at it."

"Yes—well—what do you think?" said Phyllida to the boy.

He shrugged.

"It is your treasure," he said. "My grandmother has given it to you. You can do as you wish with it."

"Oh, but you must have half," Phyllida insisted.

"For what?"

"For buying things, of course."

"What things?"

"Well—rice and cows—and knives. All the things you want."

"We have rice and cows. I have a knife. In any case we are going back to the hills, and what could we do there with gold?"

"You're going away?" they cried together. "When?"

"In a short time. When you go we shall go. We shall have more room in the hills and that is where we belong. Poo belongs there too. Poo and I are hill men, isn't it so, Poo?" and he plucked the gray figure off the branch it was swinging on and tossed it on to a higher one.

Phyllida thought of the boy, the ape, the grandmother, and the owl living together on the wooded slopes to which the parrots flew each morning; and of herself and Annabelle imprisoned in an English school; and of the temple glade grown ragged and the image black with dirt; and of Pompey, Alexander, and Lengra leafless, antless, and unloved. Surely the treasure could buy them all a place together somewhere?

"I thought of spending the money on a zoo," she said, "where we could all stay."

"Don't be stupid," said Annabelle. "What about school?"

"School!" said Phyllida gloomily. "Prison you mean. All we'll do there is eat everything that's put in front of us."

"And wear awful things like knicker linings and linen bags," added Annabelle.

"You don't wear the linen bags, silly," said Phyllida. "You put things into them."

"I know that," said Annabelle, who didn't. "But you have to wear Wellington boots and hats and garters and two aprons."

They had to explain to the boy and the grandmother what all these things were, and they said "Eesh," and "Baba," and "Ai-ee," very impressed at how much was needed for an English school. In India a slate and a piece of chalk were all that was required.

"I won't stay in any smelly old school," said Annabelle. "I shall run away."

"You won't be able to. They'll catch you and bring you back. You'll be the most unpopular girl in the school too. They'll put you into Coventry." Phyllida had read a lot of school stories about unpopular girls who ended up by being popular when they rescued the head prefect from a bull.

"I shall stow away on a ship and sail back here," said Annabelle firmly. "Unless you could turn us into parrots?" she asked the grandmother. "Just for a while, to frighten everyone so they wouldn't send us away?"

Ayah screamed and stuffed her knitting into her mouth to drown the noise.

"White peoples not. . . ." she began, but the grandmother interrupted.

"Certainly I could turn you into parrots, my darlings. Certainly, certainly, I would only need a little time, and the tongue of a lizard, and the ash of a bee burnt in a blacksmith's fire at the new moon of Chait. . . ."

"We couldn't wait that long," said Phyllida sadly. She took off one of her gym shoes and peeled the rubber from the rim with her penknife while she pondered. "Perhaps we could have the zoo somewhere near our school where we could go on weekends," she suggested.

"And we?" said the boy.

"There are hills in England," said Phyllida. But

she was beginning to feel already the hopelessness of the plan. There was silence while they all felt it.

"I shall spend my part of the treasure on horses, of course," said Annabelle. "Old ones that nobody wants. I shall train them into super show jumpers and make lots more money and buy more horses. On and on."

The boy had never heard of show jumping, and while they were in the middle of explaining it to him, Ayah shouted that it was time for them to go. So they said goodbye with the problem of the treasure still unsolved, but with Ayah happily agreeing to come every morning to the glade to meet her friend the grandmother, whom she was going to teach to knit.

"You bery naughty girls going jungle-side," she told them as they sauntered home. "Plenty tigers dat place."

"Plenty leopards too," Phyllida agreed. "I showing you plenty leopards? Spotted ones, black ones?"

"Wicked girl," Ayah giggled. "Why you teasing? I not like leopards."

"You liked the temple though? Beautiful, not?"

"Dat bery sweet snake," said Ayah, and it was such an extraordinary thing for her to say that they knew she too had fallen under the spell of the glade, and of the god whom she did not think existed.

"When we cut our rice we can have a feast there, not?" said Phyllida.

Ayah skipped with pleasure. "Lubly, lubly feasting," she agreed. "I making curry, chappattis, all tings." Then she stopped and clapped a hand to her forehead. "Mummy not liking," she said. "Mummy say dat Hindu."

"Mummy not knowing," said Annabelle.

"By then," said Phyllida, "we shall know everything."

"What dat? What you knowing?" Ayah had noticed the look they had exchanged.

"Nothing," said Annabelle. "Come on, let's run. Plenty tigers dis place."

They tore off down the path with Ayah picking up her sari and scuttling after them.

"Changing shoes," she called as they disappeared from sight. "You not taking trouble upstairs!"

She sighed and wiped the corner of her eye on her knitting. When the rice was cut the children would go, leaving her and the glade and the animals. Perhaps she would be able to take the snake to the hills with her, but she doubted it. Her aunties all hated snakes, and besides how would she manage him in the bus? She would go on to look after other children—cleaner, tidier children in white socks and hair ribbons—but never two like these.

What to do with the treasure became the second topic of conversation during the next few days. The first was the night of the full moon—Sunday night—when they must be at Brindaban for some special enchantment they knew it held.

"Full moon's super at the temple," said Phyllida so often that Annabelle said, "Honestly, you'd think you were there every night."

But they agreed on one thing: that at the full moon they must go to the temple without Ayah, and without the grandmother. For one thing Ayah would not approve of a night journey through the jungle; for another she would not believe that the blue god could appear, there or anywhere else. Annabelle did not really believe it either, but she was determined not to be left out of another adventure.

Phyllida felt Sunday approach with a mixture of excitement and awe. She knew that something wonderful and important was going to happen, but could not picture exactly what it would be. If it was the blue god in person, how would she feel meeting God, she wondered? And if she danced to his flute like the milkmaids, would her own God be betrayed? Later, at Christmas, could she return to him in his manger? She could not find the answer to her questions, nor ask for help from anyone else.

Sunday came at last and was wet. This was something they had not considered, and they stared glumly at the rain, as it poured down with a steady roar from the roof into the brick drain around the bungalow. They would not be able to see the moon if this went on, let alone dance in its light.

At teatime the rain stopped and their hill monster lay steaming in golden sunshine, circled by a rainbow. They ran onto the sodden grass of the lawn, sending up small rainbows between their toes.

"My right arm's twitching," shouted Phyllida. "A rainbow, and a twitching arm, and a full moon.

That's the luckiest you can possibly be."

They felt they needed all this luck when, hours later, they crawled out of bed and into their clothes. It was half past ten, and moonlight streamed into their bedroom window and onto their heads as they crept downstairs and out into the garden.

"The temple's s-super at the full moon," said Phyllida through chattering teeth.

"So you've said about a million times," Annabelle replied.

They crossed the paddock with their hearts thudding, and nearly jumped out of their skins when a figure stepped out from behind the gate. It was only the boy, however, and the rest of the walk to the glade was made much easier by having him there beside them, swinging his knife and talking quite naturally, as if night were no more frightening than day.

"I often walk through the jungle at this time," he said. "I can hear better, and smell better too. I can smell honey now."

"What's the use of smelling it if you can't see anything?" asked Annabelle.

"I can see," said the boy. "It is as clear as the sun, this last moon of the summer. All the animals will be out tonight, and the wild bees will have a job protecting their store."

"I suppose tigers like this sort of night?" said Phyllida, as casually as she could.

200*

"Tigers, leopards, bears, elephants," said the boy, cheerfully. "They will all be out tonight. I think they are sitting just out of reach, watching us now."

"L-lucky the L-Lord Krishna is out too," observed Phyllida, but she was glad when they reached the shelter of the temple and had lighted the butter lamps and placed their offerings of rice, saffron, and mango leaves in front of the image. Alexander was hunting, but Pompey lay moon bathing on the dappled grass. Fireflies blinked around the peepul tree and to the chirr of crickets was added the clack of frogs and the hollow boom of a long-eared owl to make the glade busy and welcoming.

"Isn't it super?" Phyllida said, quite calm and happy suddenly, and Annabelle had to admit that it was.

"But what do we do now?" she asked, when they had breathed in the night smells and admired the glitter of the moonbeams on the peepul leaves.

"Wait," said Phyllida. "Sit with our backs to the temple and wait for the blue god."

"He will be busy tonight," the boy said. "We will have to be patient."

"If he's anywhere he'll be beside the Jumna River and that's about a thousand miles from here," said Annabelle.

"*Miles?*" squeaked Phyllida. "Miles don't mean anything to gods. He can be here in a minute."

She sank onto the ground and leaned back against the temple, half closing her eyes.

"I will make him a poem while we're waiting," she announced. "A sort of welcoming song."

"If you sing you'll keep him away," said Annabelle, but Phyllida's eyes and ears were closed as she thought of the words that would be suitable to welcome a god.

"Oh thou so beautiful and blue," she droned,

"Thou the flute player,

Thou the lover of tigers and deer and anteaters and all animals both great and small."

"That line's too long," said Annabelle. "You'll have to leave out the anteaters."

"Of anteaters and all animals both great and small," Phyllida repeated firmly.

"Oh thou who killed demons,

And killed King Kamsa,

And killed all the wicked creatures of the world,

Oh thou, the blue god, we welcome thee."

"That's quite good," Annabelle admitted. "Mummy would have a fit if she heard you."

"Don't keep interrupting," Phyllida told her, "I haven't finished. That's just the introducing part."

"I've forgotten the first bit already," Annabelle complained, but Phyllida's eyes were closed again, and she was sitting with her hands joined against her chest in a gesture of welcome.

"We welcome thee," she chanted.

"Therefore leave thy milkmaids,

Leave thy dance by the Jumna River,

Tread across the white sands, and across the mountains and the jungles,

Come into this jungle, and along the path and up to our temple,

Come and play thy flute to us,

We are not afraid of the tigers if you are here, nor of the bhoots, nor of any other kind of danger."

"That's the Prayer Book." Annabelle was shocked. "You can't use that."

"He'll never come if you keep spoiling my poem," Phyllida said in her most patient voice.

"Listen," said the boy. "He is coming now."

They both sat up straight, their eyes wide, motionless in the moon's rays. Across the cricket calls, lilting and flickering like the peepul leaves, as bright as the fireflies and gentle as the night breeze, came the notes of a flute. Phyllida, who had been rescued by this same music, and comforted and led to safety, recognized it at once.

"It's him," she whispered ecstatically, triumphantly. "He's coming."

"It is him," agreed the boy. "Ai-ee, such sounds! Me, I have never heard such music."

Annabelle said nothing. Her tongue was clamped between her teeth, and her eyes popping.

Gradually the music grew stronger and its sweetness filled the glade. Pompey lifted a heavy head to listen and the fireflies seemed to swoop in time to the flute's commands. Then it was as if the gold of the moonlight paled, and turned first cream, and then blue.

It was the blue of mists, and lay on the leaves of the peepul tree like splashes of sea water. The trunk of the tree changed from gold to gray and then the same sea mist spread over it too, and over the moon-blanched grass, over Pompey, and over their own arms and knees as they sat spellbound, watching for the flute player.

Washed by the sea light the glade grew still, and the flute too. Even their own hearts seemed to have stopped beating as they sat with their azure arms on their knees, and heard the crackle of undergrowth opposite. The grass shivered and parted; there was a moment of hesitation, and then out of it, alert and bluer than a summer sky, stepped a little barking deer.

They were so surprised, expecting Krishna and getting instead a deer, that nobody could move or speak. The deer stretched its neck and moved its head from side to side questingly, ears pricked forward. Then, giving a pleased squeak, it leaped across the glade toward them.

204*

"Miranda," they said together, and leaned forward to welcome her.

"Miranda," whispered Phyllida. "You've come back. I knew you would. Oh, I'm so glad to see you, so glad, so glad."

"I too, sister deer," said the boy. "I too am glad. But where is the blue god? We are expecting him."

"He's terribly close," whispered Annabelle. They all whispered as if they were in church. "Everything's blue and still. Tell us, Miranda, where's the blue god?"

But Miranda stood with her neck stretched under their stroking hands, and then bent her head and rubbed her forehead against Phyllida's chest.

"It's the place between her horns," said Phyllida. "She likes it tickled."

Gently she pulled the soft horn buds, and with the ball of her thumb massaged the bony head between. She traced the outline of each pointed ear, running her finger tip around the familiar gap where the ear had been torn, and through the soft fur lining, familiar too.

Under Miranda's eyes were the holes which the malis said were second eyes for her to see at night. Phyllida's finger and thumb followed the grooves from forehead to dry rubbery nose, and felt the long rasping tongue explore her hand and wrist. It was so well-known, so missed, so wonderful to feel again.

She caressed the strong smooth arch of the neck, and slid her hand along Miranda's straight back and down her sides. She was fat and glossy, fatter than she had been when she lived with them.

"You're fat," she said. "You've got bulging sides."

"She will have a small deer in the spring," said the boy.

"Do you think so?" breathed Phyllida. "Yes, that must be it."

"But we won't be here in the spring," said Annabelle.

Phyllida raised her eyes to the blue glade, and with her hand still resting on Miranda's swelling side thought of the little deer that she would never see. It would have pale gold spots, as Miranda had had, and would lie here in the glade with the leaves of the peepul tree making dappled patterns on its coat.

It would see the parrots fly down from the hills, watch the cotton pods burst and send the white fluff whirling off in the March winds, hear the roar of the monsoon as it arrived to flood the rice fields, see the growing rice reflected in the flooded fields, and grow itself and lose its spots. But she would not see or hear any of these things.

The glade blurred and she rested her head against

Miranda's neck, overcome by a terrible sadness. This was where she wanted to stay forever. Leaving and losing were more than she could bear: not touching, not hearing, not seeing the things she had grown to love would be like dying. Whatever England in the spring brought her, it would not bring her Miranda's fawn, and that was all she wanted.

The blue god was close to her now, closer than he had ever been. Perhaps if she called to him, asked him to turn her into a tree, or a star—anything so that she would not have to go away. Perhaps he would come in a moment and catch Miranda, the boy, Annabelle, and herself up into some world where they could stay together and nothing would change.

As if in answer to her silent call, the notes of the flute trilled again through the glade. Phyllida looked around, Miranda's neck stretched again, and her ears pricked.

"Lord Krishna's coming," she breathed.

Then, as she listened and waited, a strange and beautiful peacefulness flowed through her. It was like the feeling she often had in the glade—as if sap were flowing through her so that she was part of the growing life around her—but this time the sap was knowledge.

It was the knowledge that there was nothing separate in the world. She and Miranda and the peepul tree were one; the boy and the python were one; and it was the same god who walked the streets of Bethlehem as carried his flute through the forests of Brindaban.

Afterward she did not know how long she had sat with her arms around Miranda's neck and the beautiful knowledge enfolding her. When she looked around at last Miranda had gone and the flute was silent and the glade no longer blue. She turned to the boy and Annabelle.

"He came," she said.

"He came," they repeated.

They did not ask each other if they had seen him; instead they talked of Miranda. It was soft, contented talk, and after half an hour they decided they must go home.

"I don't want to dig up the treasure, do you?" said Annabelle when they were back in bed again. "There's no point is there?"

"No," said Phyllida.

"It would spoil the glade," Annabelle murmured. "It must stay just as it is."

Phyllida knew then that Annabelle had felt the sap rising in her too, and that as long as they lived they would remember the full moon of the night that ended the summer.